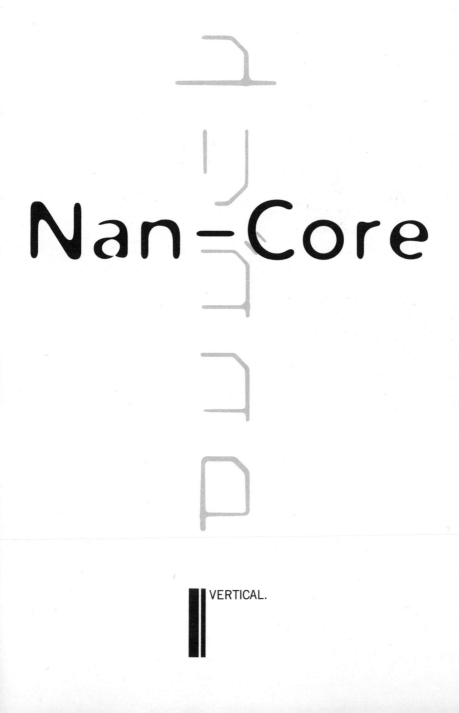

Nan-Core

VERTICAL.

Nan-Core

Mahokaru Numata

translated by Jonathan Lloyd-Davies

 VERTICAL.

Published by Vertical, Inc., New York, 2015

Originally published in Japanese as *Yurigokoro* by
Futabasha, 2011 and reissued in paperback by Futabasha, 2014.

ISBN 978-1-939130-92-1

Manufactured in the United States of America

First Edition

Vertical, Inc.
451 Park Avenue South, 7th Floor
New York, NY 10016
www.vertical-inc.com

Nan-Core

1

I decided to stop by Dad's even though it had only been three days since I'd last seen him. Black clouds rolled across the sky at a rapid pace. Sporadic squalls of wind brought down pattering raindrops that soaked, lukewarm, into my button-down shirt. It was nearly the end of July, but the rainy season seemed to have no intention of ending.

Having resigned myself to getting a little damp, I was walking unhurriedly the under-ten-minute route from the station when, for some reason, a memory from the previous winter flashed vividly into my mind: the time I had invited everyone to dinner.

It had been the beginning of December. We all gathered at Namba for an early end-of-the-year party where we dined on crabs. The "year-end party" was just an excuse; my real motivation was to bring together Chie, my parents, and my kid brother. I knew everyone would make a big fuss if I told them beforehand, so when the day came, I brought Chie along without any advance warning.

Nothing had spoiled yet, not at that point. I'm certain every last detail of that night will continue to lurk in my memories forever, enveloped in the brilliance of those last moments right before everything started to break apart.

Mom had dyed her hair a lighter shade and put on her treasured black pearl pendant. She had scooped the crab flesh out with a practiced hand, looking happy and at times earnest as she prepped enough for Dad's plate too.

Dad had been the same as ever, complaining the saké I poured went straight to his head, even though his smile made it clear he didn't mean the jab wholeheartedly.

I could tell Mom and Dad had taken a shine to Chie the moment they saw her, and I was amused watching my brother, who had gone unusually meek, try to make a good impression without being too obvious about it.

As we continued to drink and the gathering grew lively that night, there was no doubt in my mind that Chie and I would get married, that we would have children, that my parents would remain healthy, anticipating a future with grandchildren coming over to play.

That all felt like it had only been a week ago. I could very nearly smell the savory steam rising from the hot pot.

Could any of us there that day have foreseen even one of the tragedies that were to come in rapid succession almost immediately afterwards?

The first was Chie's disappearance. Less than two months had passed when it happened. With no warning at all, she stopped coming in to work and vacated her apartment.

Then, in the following spring, when I was still struggling to overcome the first surge of that shock, my Dad was diagnosed with terminal pancreatic cancer. Ironically, this became the impetus that forced me out of my constant state of obsessing over Chie.

After he learned it was inoperable, my father stubbornly

refused all drug- and radiation-based treatments. Besides, the doctors said they doubted such therapies would help, even if they forced him to take them.

We were left with no choice but to accept that Dad would soon be gone. It was only natural that everyone in the family—including Dad—steeled themselves for the inexorable progression of events that would result in him passing away before Mom.

And yet she lost her life, all too soon, in a car accident two months ago.

I had never given much thought to the existence of God or fate, but I couldn't help thinking that there was something out there, chimerical and malicious, placing spiteful traps all around me.

Another sudden squall spat rough rain and wind into my face. But the house was already visible up ahead. Between the gate and the entrance in the narrow and heavily shaded garden the stand of Nandina bamboo—no taller now than it was when I was a kid—swayed in the wind.

There was no response from inside the house after I tried pressing the intercom and knocking at the door, so I had to use my spare key. I stepped inside and noticed the house felt deserted, as though long since abandoned. I had come by a number of times when my parents had both been away, but it had never felt this vacant before. The air inside was completely transformed.

I looked around, not quite ready to venture further inside, and felt a still-raw sadness rise in my chest. The familiar single-flower vase on the shoe cupboard had a covering of chalky dust. When Mom was still alive the small glass vessel had always boasted a fresh seasonal flower. The corridor, always polished clean, had given off a subtle waxy scent. Even when no one was in the house it had felt alive, like it was breathing.

I stuck my feet haphazardly into a pair of slippers among those scattered along the entrance to the house proper and made my way down the corridor, peering into the kitchen and the bathroom as I did. When I caught sight of my tired face that I hadn't bothered shaving that morning reflected in the clouded mirror, I instinctively rubbed a hand along my cheek.

I tried searching the house, still probing my stubble with the tips of my fingers.

Where'd Dad go?

He visited Gran at the nursing home on Sundays, but it wasn't a Sunday. He had mentioned he ended up taking more aimless walks now that he was living alone, but would he really go out when the weather was this poor? It was possible that he had gone to the hospital if his condition had suddenly taken a turn for the worse.

With Mom gone and Dad in his weakened state, I knew I should move back in and live with him. One of the reasons I hadn't was because Dad didn't want me to, and because I was unable to step away from the shop I had opened a couple of years earlier that was still running on a hand-to-mouth basis.

The shop was a cafe called Shaggy Head and was located at the foot of Mt. Hachidaka. It had a one-fifth-acre playground for dogs, and I ran it on a membership-only basis for dog owners and their pets. From there it was a three-hour round trip. Counting all the housekeeping work necessary around opening and closing times, it was pretty rough.

So, for the time being, I made do with frequent visits whenever I was able to get away from work.

At one point three generations had lived together under this roof, and while the house was old it had plenty of rooms.

On entering the living room I saw that the incense stand that had been there three days earlier had been put away, leaving only the plain-wood memorial tablet and a photograph arranged on the small bureau.

The photo was of a much younger Mom, looking directly at the camera with a slightly tense smile on her face. I stood there gazing at my mother's image for a while, without even pressing my hands together. The pain had subsided but tears welled up in my eyes anyway, as if by conditioned reflex.

Force of habit carried me upstairs to keep looking even though I knew Dad was out. The floorboards groaned in places, on the stairs as well as along the second-floor corridor.

At the end I knocked, just in case, then opened the door to Dad's study, really nothing more than a small room with a large bookcase. On the low table was an ashtray with a few stubbed-out cigarettes. Dad had labored to give up smoking a decade earlier, but I guessed he'd started again, having lost any reason he'd had to abstain.

A number of books and scrapbooks were stacked towards the edge of the table, all related to worldwide projects that aided children. Even when he was young and poor, Dad had always kept up donations to a number of such organizations. He subscribed to a few newsletters and was also dedicated to collecting articles and papers about children facing poverty and abuse. Once, when I was a kid, he had found me and my younger brother looking through his scrapbooks without permission and scolded us. Come to think of it, that was the only time Dad had ever actually shouted at us; never before or since.

I decided to wait for a while in the kitchen downstairs and was just closing the door to the room when I noticed one of the sliding panels in the closet to my right was a couple inches ajar. There was something about it that piqued my interest. The closet ran the length of the wall but was halfway blocked by the bookcase and so could only be opened on one side, and therefore it was unlikely that anything but junk was stored inside.

The room was tiny but with its atmosphere of a sacred space for Dad I was wary to go in, especially in the master's absence. Regardless, I padded over to the closet and slid the door open.

Inside was a jumble of dust-covered boxes of various sizes, all in disarray as though someone had rifled haphazardly through them. One of the boxes positioned at the front of the top shelf was open, which made me think that Dad had pulled it from the back to look inside.

What had he been hoping to find? I reached inside, suddenly curious, but all that emerged was drab old clothing. To make matters worse, as soon as I pulled out the clothes from their orderly folds inside the box they became unwieldy and I realized it would be a task to get them back in as before.

Seeing nothing else for it I hauled the box to the floor and had begun fumbling around to get the contents back in order when I found a musty old handbag buried at the bottom. It was something a married woman might use. It was white and designed for use during the summer.

I initially assumed it had to be one of Mom's, but when I took it in my hands and looked it over I felt an inexplicable sense of foreboding. *It's not hers*, I decided, not knowing the source of my sudden flash of conviction.

I had never seen it before, yet it was familiar. An oddly distorted sensation crawled up from the bag, from the leather that had yellowed over time, from the rust-speckled metal of the clasp. I felt my body threaten to start trembling.

I was hit with an urge right then to put the bag back into the box and shut the lid tight, but that brought with it a mysterious pang of guilt. I used the back of my hand to wipe the sweat that had beaded up on my forehead, and, with trembling fingers, gently undid the clasp.

Inside was a small packet made of *washi* paper. The napped surface of the paper bore an inscription in faint black ink: Misako.

Carefully opening the packet, I found a bundle of hair, black, about two inches long.

Goosebumps broke out all over my skin.

It was—it had to be—a keepsake, hair from someone that had died.

Misako was Mom's name, and her funeral had been held only two months earlier. But the hair was jet black without a single strand of white, so it couldn't have been from then. If it was Mom's it was something taken years ago, back when she had still been young. But who would have done that, and for what reason? Why prepare something like this, so long before her actual death?

I felt a deep sense of something sinister.

If Mom had died from an illness, perhaps then I would

have been less agitated. I realized in hindsight that she had been acting strangely in her final month. She would sometimes nod along to a conversation but not actually understand it, and she would occasionally burst into tears in the middle of watching coverage of distressing incidents on the news.

One time I caught sight of her when I was on my way home from the train station. I had happened to glance back and seen her walking towards me, coming home with some shopping. I will never forget her face—she had looked terrified, like an empty shell. Mom was only a few years into her fifties but that time she had looked gray and worn out, like an old woman. I instinctively turned my gaze away, feeling as though I'd witnessed something forbidden. It had seemed like the face of another side of her, a side she would never have willingly revealed to Dad or me. When she noticed me she seemed to panic momentarily, but then her usual smile quickly returned and she called out, sounding happy: "Oh hello, Ryo dear!"

When I reached out to relieve her of the supermarket bags she carried in both hands I looked down and noticed she was shuffling along in Dad's sandals. They were too big for her feet and her socks stuck out, blackened from dirt where the tips touched the ground. At the time I read nothing more into it, telling myself it was all due to Dad's illness, that she was just upset because of it. And, perhaps, that was actually all it was.

Two months ago Mom and Dad had been on their way back from seeing Gran. Dad said they'd been standing side by side at a red light at a crosswalk when Mom stepped out into the road without warning.

"By the time I managed to shout out she was already gone, nowhere to be seen. I couldn't even grasp what just happened. I don't remember hearing any of it, not the collision, not the squeal of brakes, not the noise of people around us. I just stood there, watching everyone running about in confusion around the truck right in front of me like I was watching a silent movie."

On the night of the funeral the two of us sat in the kitchen when Dad told me this, and it was as if he was mostly talking to himself. Our unspoken mutual understanding was that he would be dead too, before long. My brother fell into a drunken sleep after reaching that dazed, cried-out place. But Dad did not weep or abandon himself to heartrending grief, not for the accident that had taken his wife, not for his own impending death. Instead his eyes contained something elusive, not sadness or fear but something pale and dry. I could only describe it as an emptiness.

As we sat facing each other, unable to find words to share, I began to suspect it had been nesting inside him from before I could remember, that I had been dimly aware of it the whole time. I recalled Dad sitting hunched over the low table in his study, lost as always in page after page of the scrapbooks he had filled with so many photographs. Children with sarcomas dotting their faces, ravaged by AIDS; emaciated kids, the shape of their bones visible through their skin; small, naked corpses, abused and discarded... Maybe it's strange for me, his own son, to say, but there was always something a little eccentric about Dad.

I gazed at the bundle of black hair in my hand for a few more moments, then wrapped it back up in the paper. I didn't know what else to do.

I had just popped the clasp shut, having put the parcel back into the handbag, when a memory sprang into my mind like a jack-in-the-box bursting open. It came rushing back, something that had for some reason been absent from my memories for a very long time. Yet it was crystal clear, as though it had never slipped from my mind at all.

I was four at the time, so this had happened over twenty years ago. I had spent a long while in hospital with pneumonia or something like that and when I finally got home after being discharged I had become convinced that my mother had been replaced by someone else.

If not for seeing the bundle of hair, I doubt the memory would have ever resurfaced for the rest of my life. Of course, it was absurd to have thought that someone had taken Mom's place, so this curious memory would have most likely remained dormant, existing as nothing more than a child's illusion, consigned to the dark recesses of my mind along with so many other recollections.

I was told that, during my stay in the hospital, there had been a small fire at our rented apartment. That incident had spurred my parents to move from Tokyo to Komagawa in Nara, where they bought a house to share with my grandparents who were going to move in from Maebashi.

On the day of my discharge I rode the bullet train back with Dad, switching partway to the Kintetsu Line, and by the time we finally pulled into Komagawa I was exhausted, feeling like I'd traveled all the way to the edge of the world. I became utterly bewildered when I walked into the recently-constructed and unfamiliar house and saw Mom run up to the entryway and call out, "Ryo, you're back!"

No, I thought, *you're not my Mom.*

"You're such a strong boy, Ryo! Mommy's so sorry she couldn't come to visit you," she said, hugging me close, her eyes wet with tears. I stiffened, feeling awkward in the embrace.

Of course I tried to explain this to Dad and my grandparents, even to Mom herself. "What happened to my Mom?" I would ask. But the adults only laughed. They wouldn't take me seriously, teasing that I'd forgotten what she looked like after not seeing her during the months in hospital.

I had a feeling that Mom might have visited once, not too long after my admission to the hospital, but I couldn't be sure. Coming to visit was solely Dad's job. Even after the move he had stayed back in Tokyo, living out of a business hotel not far from the hospital and his work. He'd quit the job once I was out of the hospital.

I have a vague memory of him explaining how it was difficult for Mom to visit me at the hospital—I had probably been complaining about wanting to see her—explaining it was because we had moved far away, and since Gran was in bad health she had to look after her.

So it was true that I hadn't seen her for a while. In addition, I had come home to a strange place that wasn't the home I'd known before the hospital, to a town and a house I'd never seen before and where my grandparents who had until then lived on their own had moved in as well. Thinking back, it was probably enough to wreak havoc with a child's perceptions, and it wasn't surprising for me to think Mom looked like someone else.

Yet that sense of wrongness was deep-rooted, like something that went beyond simple reasoning. And even when the casual dismissal of the adults had begun to convince me that maybe they were right, that maybe she was Mom after all, all the while the sense of something being out of place continued to throb, like a milk tooth that was loose but wouldn't quite come out.

I had a hard time calling her "Mom," this person that should have been my mother. There was nothing different about the way she acted around me. She would hug me tenderly when I wanted her to, and throw a fit when I did something very bad. I still couldn't call her "Mom," but it didn't take long to grow attached, either.

I have a few fragmented memories from that time. One time, my mother took me to a bookstore and found a picture book which she bought for me. It was one of my favorites before I was admitted to the hospital—the story was about a terrifying, man-eating dragon—but it had burned in the fire along with my other books and toys. She called out in surprise and picked up the book with an air of nostalgia and smiled at me, and I happily noted a sudden surge in the conviction that she might really be my mother after all. When I got home I was disappointed to page through the book and find that the man-eating dragon that had been so terrifying to look at before was actually not scary at all. If anything, it looked comical. When I told as much to my mother she patted me on the head and said, "You poor thing, Ryo. All sorts of things must seem different to you now after being in hospital for so long and putting up with so many ouchie needles."

Another time, my mother licked free some grit that had

got stuck in my eye. She assured me it would be fine and, although my eyelid was jammed shut from the pain, it relaxed naturally when she placed her tongue over it. I remember the sensation even now, of her tongue being neither hot nor cold, just soft. She took my head in her hands and directly licked my eyeball with her tongue. The relief stopped my tears, and I remembered then how she had used the same technique to clean dirt from my eyes when I had been smaller. When she was done I asked her how it tasted and she said, "Ryo, your tears are very salty."

I wondered what else I could have done, during those days filled with such tiny moments.

At some point—at least, this is what seems likely—the discomfort I felt towards my mother came to be replaced by guilt for still feeling that way. And you don't need much effort to forget guilt, especially when you're a child. By the time my brother Yohei was born a year later, I had completely forgotten about the doubts I had had regarding my mother. Back then her hair had been black and glossy, without as much as a single strand of white...

I let my eyes fall once more to the handbag still in my hands.

A vague image floated to mind: a woman in a sleeveless dress printed with large flowers, and this handbag resting on her arm. I couldn't decide whether the image was of my mother before she was replaced or simply a fictitious picture that I had invented.

I didn't even know whether it was true or not that she had been replaced.

I sat cross-legged on the tatami flooring, lost for a while

in a daze. Eventually I pulled myself together and dug further into the box I'd pulled the handbag from. It wasn't clear if it had been there from the outset, or if Dad had pulled something else out to hide it, but right at the bottom I found a manila envelope stuffed with papers of some sort, or documents. I opened it to find a collection of notebooks. There were four in total, each a different thickness and design. Each had a number written in the bottom-right corner of the cover, one through four.

I chose one and flipped through it. The pages were crammed full of text, leaving hardly any blank spaces. The sentences were written in heavy pencil, with occasional scuffs where an eraser had been used. The characters were artlessly scrawled across the page, but there was no way to tell if the style was put on or just the author's natural hand.

I took out the notepad marked One and began to read. Nan-Core was written in as the title. I didn't know what it meant. My hand was throwing shadows onto the page so I moved closer to the window. Before long the text sucked me in, and I forgot everything else around me.

2

Nan-Core

Is it an abnormality in my brain structure that allows people like me to kill so easily?

I heard that there is a complex interaction between the many hormones in the brain, that even a small change in that balance can have a large effect on mood and personality. That was when the idea occurred to me that, if medical research in the field continued to progress, perhaps there might one day be a drug that could cure the urge to kill.

If a medicine like that existed, I think I would try taking it.

I kill people because I want to. I've never felt anything like guilt. But if something came along that was able to stop me from doing it I think I'd try it regardless. I don't know why. It's strange, even to me.

I don't know where to start. Maybe the warning signs, the trigger that made me the way I am… I hope I'll be able to explain them properly. When I was around four or five, my mother began taking me on regular visits to the hospital. The doctor would always press his fingers over the small lump on the back of my head, then he would take out picture cards and watch as he slowly repeated words like "apple, apple, apple." It was only much later that I realized he had wanted me to say "apple," too. I don't know if it was somehow related to the lump on my head, but while I could more or less understand what people were saying to me, back then I never tried to say anything in response.

My examination was always over quickly, but once it was done my mother would spend a long time talking to the doctor about what I was like at home. The bespectacled doctor always spoke in a hushed tone. My mother would talk, sometimes through tears, and he would listen and nod patiently, rejoindering with a muttered explanation when necessary.

One of the things he said quite often in an apologetic tone was something like, "Your child doesn't have … Nan-Core, so I'm afraid it can't be helped." The "…" part of his explanation would sometimes change and I don't remember all the variations, but his point was that there were many types of Nan-Core and that I had none of them.

Other times the doctor would say things like, "Not having Nan-Core is a big problem," or "It'd be great if we could find a suitable type of Nan-Core for your child." I was just a kid, but it felt unfair all the same. Why did I have to be missing something everyone else had? There was always a vague thought in my mind that I somehow had to get myself a Nan-Core.

On our way back from the hospital my mother would take me to various places on her errands, and this would cause me unbearable pain. I was used to the hospital, but each time I went somewhere for the first time it felt like all the new things were stabbing me with a mass of invisible thorns.

The place I felt most relaxed was in my room at home, wedged into the gap between my bed and the wall. I would sleep there each time I had a fit, and my mother would bring my food up to me.

One day after an examination, my mother took me to a bargain hall inside a department store. Immediately the hustle and bustle, the colors and smells bore down on me. I followed in silence wherever she led me by the hand, and I don't think she or anyone else could have realized that I was completely terrified and had almost wet myself (I had in fact wet myself a few times before). If my doctor had touched the lump at the back of my head during times like this, I think that instead of finding it soft as usual he would have found it swollen and hard.

At first my mother kept a tight grip on my hand, then she let go for a moment to spread out some clothes she had picked from the mountain of items on special sale and from then onwards kept taking my hand then letting go again. After she did this a few times I stole away and left the jam-packed bargain hall behind me.

Along the wall past the escalators was an area with only a few people milling about among displays of upright clocks, vases, and various metal fixtures whose uses I couldn't begin to understand. Looking back now I suppose it was an antique fair.

I walked closer and immediately noticed a small girl inside one of the glass showcases. She was blond and staring at me with a look that was something like surprise or resignation. In the moment our eyes met all the floods of color and attacking noises were washed away by silence, as if by magic. I knew then and there that she was my Nan-Core. It was there, in such a place. Something I had never expected to find.

I knew it was going to be okay.

After a while my mother came looking for me. I had camped down in front of the showcase and wouldn't budge even when she pulled my hand.

"What? You want a doll?" mother asked. I think she was surprised, because that was the first time I'd ever refused to listen or acted like I wanted something. She eyed the price tag and muttered to the seller about how it looked old and worn, seemingly unconvinced as she considered it, but she ended up buying Nana (as I was already calling her in my mind; the name felt natural) for me. Perhaps she bought the doll because the doctor had told her each time we visited the hospital that the best thing was to let me do what I wanted.

As an aside: When my mother was pregnant with me she once slipped getting onto the bus and fell, hitting her abdomen hard on the edge of one of the steps. As a result, she was convinced it was her fault that I didn't speak.

The package that came with Nana contained a few different outfits and a miniature baby bottle. Nana was an old resin doll, designed to drink milk. Her eyelashes were long and grouped in bunches, planted around blue eyes that clicked shut when she lay flat. Her tiny lips were painted with red enamel and had a short round tube for drinking milk embedded in the center. I couldn't help but think the tube made her expression look a little startled, like she was caught in the moment before a scream.

When we got home, and as soon as it was just Nana and me in the space between the bed and the wall, I just had to pry off her frilly clothes, made of dark red velvet, and pull down her rough cotton underwear to see below. Her underbelly was gently swollen and had the same thin tube as the one in her mouth sticking through the middle. It felt incredibly lewd. Not that I understood such concepts at the time, of course. I brought my face up to the pipe and peered into her, but the only thing I could make out through the narrow opening was a gloomy darkness.

Even so I knew that, at her core, Nana was my Nan-Core.

That I was saved.

I played with her every day. I remember all the details vividly, like something from a morbid dream. I would stand her up, naked, as I used the baby bottle to pour water through the tube in her mouth. Her eyes would stay wide open as the liquid dripped from her underbelly, and the whole time she maintained a befuddled expression. After this I would turn her rosy, chubby figure upside down. Her legs would spin down from the crotch and catch at an impossible angle, fully exposing the tiny secret between them. The end of the tube inside her protruded a bit at the end. I would carefully attach the bottle to this, and pour more water in.

I was Nana. I was an empty vessel. I was unable to close off the pipe that was open inside me. I had no means to stop the things that flowed into or out of me. Nana's fears were my own, and my fears were hers. When upside down, her eyes would clamp shut as the water flowed relentlessly, out from her little bird-like mouth, soaking her hair.

My mother watched me with a discomfited look as I did little besides play with the doll. But I never got bored. The doll's blond hair was always soaking wet. Eventually, after a while of repeating the game over and over, I sensed a small change occurring within me. It felt as though I was gradually building up an immunity against both the outside world and myself.

I realized I probably wouldn't fall to pieces if I spoke a little.

Despite my mother's misgivings, I was admitted to regular classes in elementary school. I had learned to give simple, short verbal responses barely moving my lips at all. The lump at the nape of my neck no longer stood out.

Even so, I still went through my days feeling like half my brain was unconscious. I stared vacantly with wide-open eyes as I took in the world around me. I was still just like Nana. I can see it even now. Since I could first remember, I had always lived with my own peculiar sense of discomfort. It's hard to put into words. The feeling was like licking sandpaper or wearing a terribly itchy, wooly sweater on bare skin… I don't know. Everything around me was frizzled and sharp-edged, hostile in some unidentifiable way.

Amongst all this the adults were the most overpowering. Their physical size, their smells, their words, facial expressions, the way they laughed—it all pressed down on me with particular force. My classmates seemed distant and incomprehensible, too, in the way they would chat so effortlessly with these terrifying grown-ups.

When I was in second grade there was a girl in my class called Michiru, and she was really bright. She was pretty and from a well-off home; she was the Queen Bee, the sort found in every classroom.

I don't know why, but she alone became very special to me.

The kids from our class always used to go over to her house to play. Michiru's inner circle was made up of the same three girls, and beyond that was a group of hangers-on of about a dozen girls and boys.

I could only watch on from the periphery, of course, but Michiru was magnanimous enough not to mind when I mixed in and tagged along with the others to her house. Even better, when our eyes met every now and again, she would go so far as to flash a smile or give me a nod.

Although they weren't quite the same as Nana's, Michiru had wonderfully long eyelashes. Her house had once belonged to the old village headman and the old-fashioned, single-story wooden structure was surrounded by a large, tree-filled garden. There was a pond ringed with stones beside which stood a wisteria trellis, under which was a ceramic table surrounded by several stools. That area formed the mainstay for games of make-believe or hide and seek. When Michiru and the three girls of her entourage sat there a couple of the stools would still be free, and there were always small fights over who would join them.

I never considered sitting there myself. I was never given a role to play during make-believe games and no one tried to find me when we played hide and seek. But no one really bullied me either. I didn't feel much of anything either way.

One day when the others were passing around comics I was crouched a short distance away, watching a snail that had attached itself to an azalea leaf. The snails in the expansive grounds of Michiru's large home were big enough to be creepy, almost as fat as a loquat fruit. Next to me was an old, abandoned well, plugged with a round, wooden lid. I found a small gap where part of the rim had rotted away, just small enough that a clenched fist wouldn't fit through. I was afraid something like a snake might crawl out, but I couldn't resist the urge to get in closer and take a peek. I felt a compulsion to look. It was as if the gap had found me and not the other way around.

I stepped closer and a musty, dark scent wafted up. I sucked in the dank smell on an inhalation. The moment I pressed my face to the gap, darkness clung to my eyes. I couldn't tell where my eyes ended and the dark began. It was just endlessly, totally dark.

I forgot I was in a garden in the middle of the day. There were beads of sweat on my back.

"Death." I don't remember if the word actually came into my head right then, but it was apparent to me that the darkness stretching out into the depths of that well was boundless compared to the bright outside world.

I felt like I would be sucked in headfirst if I didn't do something. I doubted anyone would notice if I went missing. I finally managed to peel my face away and rushed over to where I had been watching the snail. It was gross but I made myself pull at the shell until the creature came off the leaf and rolled into my palm.

I dropped the snail through the gap.

Without a sound the whirlpool-patterned shell and its contents were immediately swallowed by the darkness. It was as though it had become a part of the abyss.

I felt a little calmer. Because, for that day at least, I felt that I had managed to avoid being sucked through the hole.

From that day onwards, it became my secret task to drop bugs through the hole whenever I went to Michiru's place. It felt like a duty I was obliged to perform, or even a mission from God (all children have a part of them that instinctively believes in such things). Snails were easy to catch, but it didn't really matter what I used. Earwigs, worms, even cicada that were too weak to move. When everyone else was raising hell playing statues, I would be off to the side, crawling through the garden searching for tiny creatures.

The more I dropped into the darkness, the more addicted I became, a slave to the mysterious delight the act elicited. Kindness welled up inside me, and even though I really knew that dropping the bugs down the hole meant they would die, it felt rather like I was helping the snails and worms get back to where they belonged. Because there was nothing glaring or sharp in the dark world beyond the hole, only silence.

I felt a peace of mind, knowing I was doing something that

needed to be done. All I had to do was send through enough lives, and a safe balance could be maintained.

It was the first time I had started something of my own accord, with a clear sense of purpose. I also felt a strong sense of superiority over the other kids, who were ignorant, lost in child-like games.

I was in the garden as usual one day—the wisteria petals had fallen to the ground around the trellis, so I think it was early summer—when suddenly the sky turned dark and it began to drizzle. Michiru suggested that everyone go indoors for some snacks, but I didn't budge from the garden even as everyone else raised a clamor as they headed to the house. For some reason I had yet to catch a single bug that day and hadn't sent a single offering through the hole. It had never happened before and I was worried that something bad would happen if I didn't fix the situation quickly.

I had just found a small tree frog and was in the middle of chasing it when it started to rain. It was hopping about frantically and when I finally managed to grab it I caught sight of a red polka-dot umbrella just past a low fence.

It was Michiru. She was walking right towards me. I jumped to my feet.

"Oh, you're still out here?" she asked, without any apparent surprise. "Hey, I left my hat somewhere around here. I'd hate for it to get wet. Have you seen it?" she asked mildly, tilting her head. It was as though the fact that I couldn't speak like a normal kid didn't bother her at all.

I froze in terror. All I could do was shake my head violently. I had never been alone with her before.

"What's that?" She drew even closer. I shaped my hands into a bowl to hold the frog in. "A… fr…frog," I said through clenched teeth. So long as my teeth were shut tight I was okay.

"What? A frog? You're okay with touching something like that? Wow!" She sounded genuinely impressed. "Did you catch it yourself? What kind is it? Let me see. C'mon, let me see. I know! Let's let it swim in the pond," Michiru said breezily as she skipped over the low flat stones that lined the pond.

I jerked my way over to her, as requested, then slightly pulled back my hand that had been acting as a lid covering the frog. As I did so, the frog, which had been docile until then, perhaps startled by the sudden light, sprang towards Michiru's shoulder.

A short shriek and a splash sounded out in unison as Michiru lurched backwards and tumbled into the pond. The red umbrella flew all the way to the middle and flipped upside-down, floating on the surface.

It wasn't a deep pond. I don't really know how, but one of Michiru's socks got caught up in the branches of a bush at the edge of the pond, and due to this she was unable to get up from the position she landed in—facing the sky with her head below the rest of her. With just one leg sticking out from the water, she could do nothing but writhe.

I could tell she was screaming under the water. I couldn't hear a thing, but there were lots of bubbles. I just stood there as the water churned, my mind devoid of any thoughts, eyes wide open.

Michiru's thin leg was right there before me, and I could see the pointed branch poking through the white fabric of her sock. If I took off her sneaker and her sock, she could have escaped from the pond in no time. In some remote part of my mind, I was aware of this. And yet I stayed as I was, just watching as Michiru thrashed in the water. It might have been that I was simply overwhelmed by the sheer abnormality of the scene. I had no ill will towards her.

The water suddenly went still, as though the frantic splashing hadn't actually happened. When the bubbles cleared I saw Michiru, her hair swaying within the greenish water.

I felt a surge of relief, and smiled at Michiru. This was because she looked relieved, too. Her eyes and mouth were open beneath the water.

I thought that she had gone through the hole in place of the frog she had let escape, that her soul had left her body and gone on by itself to dissolve into the darkness on the other side. Then I left through the back gate I often used and went home.

The adults and the other kids all cried over Michiru's death, thinking it an unfortunate accident.

I retraced it all in my mind, again and again. In the short moments that led up to her death, my usual sense of discomfort melted away, and everything seemed pure and bright, all the trees and stones in the garden, the sky and the whole world beyond it. Mysteriously, I could sense that that was the true form of the world. It felt like a miracle to be standing there, right in the center of the world as it really was. The sensation lasted only until the pond grew quiet.

After the funeral, everyone stopped going to Michiru's house to play. Sometime later I hugged Nana, the first time I had done so in a while. She had become an elderly woman even though she was still a girl. The red enamel on her lips was faded and patches of her blond hair had come out, revealing her scalp and the pimple-like holes where the bunches had been inserted.

I dropped Nana from a stone bridge into the dirty river that ran by my house. Her arms jutted into the air as she floated away, the thin, white, cord-like reeds that covered the riverbed brushing against her back.

Nobody would pour water through her anymore. She would

flow through the water as it would flow through her, all the way to the ocean, to a deep, dark hole at its floor.

I threw my doll away because the feeling I'd had when Michiru was dying had become my Nan-Core.

In a world full of hostility like shards of glass, I came to think of myself as special, someone who had been selected to protect a special secret. I still didn't speak much, but my new, warped sense of confidence allowed me to talk normally with my classmates in middle school. The bodies of the other boys and girls all gave off an odor like raw fish, and I knew that mine did, too. But while they were drawn towards sweet things like romance, my desire was, needless to say, only for Nan-Core.

I want to experience that again. That was the only thought I couldn't shake from my mind. I desperately yearned for it again, that miraculous light that had touched me only while the greenish water of the pond had churned. The well in Michiru's garden had opened a deep, pitch-black void in my chest before I'd even noticed.

So I waited, impatient for the next sacrificial offering to appear. I didn't understand why, and there was nothing I could do to stop myself. I suppose all I can say is, that's just the sort of person I am. And if it wasn't for a series of insignificant coincidences, I might have anxiously craved it for the rest of my life. Even now I believe that might have been a strong possibility. Yet on a Sunday nearing summer vacation during my freshman year of high school, the cogs of chance snapped together in such a way that made it seem more like someone's design than mere happenstance.

I was sitting on a bench in the park near the train station, reading a book. There was an unseasonably cool breeze, and the park was bustling with people. I looked up for no reason in particular, and saw a couple of kids that appeared to be brother and sister running, hand in hand, down one of the paths towards me. Unwittingly, I gave a small cry from shock—from her age, to the straight hair that fell on her shoulders, it was startling just how much the girl resembled Michiru.

3

The first notebook abruptly ended there.

I panted as I downed deep breaths. It felt as though I had been so absorbed in reading that I'd forgotten to breathe at all. Confused and puzzled, I ended up gazing meaninglessly at the notebook's cover.

What is this thing? It was clearly pretty old from the way the paper had yellowed. Based on the fact that the author had grown attached to a doll it made me think it was written by a woman—at the same time, however, the mother was also described as being considerably uncomfortable with it, which could imply that she thought, *It's ridiculous for a boy to be playing with dolls.*

I wondered if Dad had written it. It could have been a draft for a novel. Dad had worked in the field of accounting his whole life, right up until two years ago when the logistics company he worked for went bankrupt. I had never seen him read a novel or anything of the sort. The shelves in the study were evidence of that—apart from a handful of papers illuminating the human rights issues of children, they were mostly stuffed with books on finance or taxes, with a few on ancient Japanese history that covered things like the mysteries of the country of Yamatai and Queen Himiko, and a couple of journals on frontier-land travels.

Of course, that didn't mean it was impossible for him to have written it. Maybe he'd written it out of some unexpected interest but kept it hidden from the family out of shyness.

I concentrated on things like that, trying to convince myself they were true. I swallowed, trying to tamp down a swell of anxiety.

By the time I realized what I was doing, I had already started reading the second notebook.

I watched the girl and I knew I was staring at her with an unnatural intensity. I called out silently from my heart—*Michiru, Michiru*—and of course they walked straight past, neither the girl nor her brother noticing.

There was a grouping of vending machines ahead on the path that circled the park, so I wondered if they might be going there to get a drink. I still don't know if that was the case, as they never made it that far.

Instinct pulled me to my feet, and I began to follow them.

How small and frail they all seemed to me, girls the age Michiru and I had been back then.

Just as I began to follow them the girl stopped abruptly, deciding for some reason to put on the white hat that she had been carrying. As she did this a sudden gust of wind caught the hat as if it had been waiting to do so all along. The hat sailed into the air then fell into a gutter between the park and the road. The gutter had an iron grate covering it, reddish with rust, and it was just a stroke of bad luck that the hat had slipped underneath. The siblings cried out in dismay, as did a young man sitting on a bench nearby.

"You idiot. Hey, it's not my fault. Mom's gonna be mad," the boy said, stepping over the low fence that bordered the park to peek into the gutter. Despite his spiteful tone, it looked like he wanted to get the hat back for her.

The young man appeared preoccupied with watching them, so I sat down on an empty bench next to him.

"Can you reach it?" The girl was nearly in tears.

"Eww, gross. It's full of junk. Ah! I see it, it's caught down there."

The boy stuck a hand through the grate and tried rummaging around. He grit his teeth and pushed his arm through to the shoulder, but the hat was still out of reach.

The young man who had been watching them got to his feet.

"Hey kid, lemme take a look for you." He moved the boy aside and peered down but immediately said, "Oh, it looks too far to reach, even for an adult."

When he said this, the girl standing by the gutter began to sob aloud. The man, at a complete loss, dragged his fingers through his unkempt hair that hung nearly to his shoulders. After considering for a while he crouched down and gripped the edge of the iron grate, then he tensed, grunting as he lifted it up a good four inches. He lowered it back down and exhaled noisily.

Though still hazy and shapeless, an idea of what could happen floated into my mind. My interest had shifted from the girl that looked like Michiru; now I was fascinated with the boy. The gaping maw of the dark well in my chest was stretched open, desperate for him.

"All right, I'll pull up the grate, you grab the hat as fast as you can, okay? Go round that way—okay, get ready…"

The man stepped into the gutter and strained, using both hands to pull up one side of the grate while the boy, already waiting on his stomach, lowered his torso through the gap.

"Can you go a little higher, mister? Just a little…uff…a little further."

I could see the man's back from where I was. His muscles were bunched tight, trembling slightly around his shoulders and the back of his neck. I had no idea how heavy the grate was, but it was about two feet wide and over three feet long.

"Hey, kid… H-Hurry it up…"

"Ah, I just touched the edge, I'm almost there…"

A muffled groan came from the man's throat, but he couldn't form words.

I got up from the bench and started to move closer, holding my breath but walking normally.

The boy's thin neck.

I was almost choking on the anticipation welling up inside me. Everything I could see around the dark hole had started to shimmer with radiant light: the park, the power lines, the sky. The creature called my self awakened. The new reality was so vivid it stung, and I wanted to suck it dry.

"Ng, uugh…"

The man gave another loud groan and I saw the boy's legs scrape restlessly against the ground. I didn't know if he had finally reached the hat or if it was the man's grunting scaring him, but either way he was trying to wriggle out of the gap. The man holding the grate must have seen this, too. I could tell he was summoning his last reserves of strength for a final, desperate push, probably thinking the ordeal was almost over.

Now—

Making it look like I was trying to help, like I couldn't bear to merely stand by and watch, I took the edge of the grate in both hands. I was full of Nan-Core. I felt drunk but also sharply alert, both sensations ruling my consciousness without contradiction.

I tensed my muscles, pretending to lift the grate while actually pushing it down. In fact, I hardly needed to put any effort into it at all. The man's strength was already at its limit—it only took a slight nudge for his grip to fail.

There was the sound of the grate coming down. Then the boy's legs jerked unnaturally, convulsing. It was over in a second.

The echoes of sound quickly died out, giving rise to an emptiness that made it feel like time had stopped. The man sat on his heels and the young girl was still standing as both stared vacantly at the inert legs on the asphalt. The thin, childish legs made the sneakers on his feet look disproportionately rugged.

A crowd began to form. After some time I got to my feet and walked away.

I wondered whether the man would argue his defense. Whether he would say his failure to hold on was because of a passerby, that someone had pushed down on the grate out of malice. That as a result, it wasn't his fault the kid had died. Or did he not even realize what had happened in that moment?

I ran these thoughts through my mind as I walked down the path. When I got to the vending machines I slipped some coins into one of the slots, hoping to soothe my parched throat.

After reading this far, I sank weakly to the ground from where I had been leaning against the window frame.

I couldn't keep reading. There was a dull nausea wriggling in my stomach, and I had broken out a greasy sweat.

What are *these? What are they doing in our house?* I kept telling myself to calm down, but I only began to fret more and more. I rubbed my hands vigorously over my face, wondering semi-seriously if I was dreaming. If it wasn't a dream it had to be something Dad had written. Something he had tried for fun when he was young, something he had forgotten about. He had probably come across the notebooks when sorting his things, but hesitant to throw them out, had shoved them into a box instead.

That must have been it. After all, what other possibilities were there?

I couldn't imagine someone as placid as Mom writing them. And it didn't make sense to hold on to them if they were someone else's work. My parents weren't sociable people, they weren't close enough to anyone to do that.

Nothing to get worked up about.

I repeatedly muttered this to myself and tried to continue reading, but the chill was still there, crawling up from the pit of my stomach. I couldn't see why I was getting so shaken up. What was it that made me think it was Dad's diary, that it was a confessional text based on fact? When I'd normally skim through this kind of thing without a second thought, certain that it was fiction. When no son worth the name would suspect his father in this way.

Still crouching down, I took two, then three, deep breaths, waiting for the chills to subside. My head was spinning with doubts that shouldn't have been doubts at all. That childhood memory of Mom being replaced by someone else... Was it true after all? And if so, what happened to my real mother afterwards? Who was the woman I'd always thought of as my mother?

What was the significance of that bundle of hair?

I was afraid. I couldn't get rid of the feeling that the notebooks would contain information about my first mother. That the mother who'd left had been murdered, that they would explain in detail both why and how it had happened.

Right now, I could put the notebooks back in the bottom of the box, shut the closet doors, and pretend none of this had happened. The option was there. If I was lucky, I might, over time, come to think of what I had already read as pure fiction, perhaps even forget about it completely. But I knew that was impossible, that I had to read them to the end, no matter how miserable they might make me or how much I might come to regret it.

Once I graduated high school, I happened to end up in a two-year course at a technical school. While I was still far from sociable, I had a much better understanding of the difference between behavior that stuck out as odd and behavior that appeared normal, and as a result I was able to live while blending in seamlessly among other people.

When I was with other students, who knew nothing about Nan-Cores as they worried over future careers or dreamed of relationships, I remember feeling a mix of powerful superiority and melancholic envy.

I knew the word "Nan-Core" didn't really exist, of course. I had realized that a long time ago, probably when I was in my fifth or sixth year of elementary school.

I think my childhood doctor had actually said "an anchor." He had said I lacked a "sensory" or "cognitive" or "emotional" anchor.

He used to push up his glasses and mumble, and my young ears couldn't catch what he said too well, but even so it seemed a strange thing to mishear.

It wasn't a problem by that point, though. The word had laid roots inside me, become something that was mine alone. I couldn't correct it, there was nothing to be done about it. It expressed everything I lacked in my day-to-day life, all the things that were otherwise impossible to put into words. What other word out there can describe the inexplicable phenomenon that occurs when someone's life fades away?

It was, incidentally, in my second year in elementary school that the hospital visits stopped. During my last examination my mother asked the doctor whether the lump at the back of my head would continue to shrink, and even disappear one day.

"I'm afraid it's impossible to predict. It's an extremely rare condition, so there's a great deal we don't know about it. To be honest, I'd like to do an autopsy just to see what's going on in there."

My mother cried that night as she related the story to Dad. We stopped going after that; she couldn't forgive the doctor for the insensitivity he had shown in talking about an autopsy of a child that was still alive.

While I spent all of my time concentrating on keeping myself from standing out, a chance encounter led me to be on speaking terms with one particular girl. Our eyes first met when she was stealing something from a market near school.

Let's say her name was Mitsuko.

I was walking towards the back to get a bottled drink when I saw her shoving a bag of candy up the sleeve of her sweater from the overloaded shopping basket on her arm. This girl had made a bit of a name for herself in school because she was so thin she looked like she was recovering from some illness, and because she wore make-up so thick it made everyone do a double-take. She was always alone and never spoke to anyone, and whatever she did, whether it was just walking or sitting down, she did it so awkwardly that it seemed like she suffered from tunnel vision.

She didn't seem to panic when she saw me; she even gave me a little grin. I found myself grinning back, and pointed out a security mirror in the corner of the ceiling. She was clearly standing in full view of the register.

With sluggish movements, she pulled out several bags of candy, aside from the one she'd just been squirreling up her sleeve, and put them back into her overflowing basket.

"You getting something? A drink?" Her voice was surprisingly limpid. She could speak just like anyone else.

I nodded, taking a plastic bottle from the shelf.

"Just that? Come on, then. This one's on me."

There was an apathetic youth manning the register, and I suspected he would have turned a blind eye even if he had caught her shoplifting.

I hadn't really been interested in her before, but I had for a while felt that Mitsuko and I were something like kindred spirits. I wondered if the theatrical, mask-like coating of makeup she wore was the flip side of whatever force it was that compelled me to remain hidden. The familiarity she had just displayed might, I mused, be because she sensed the same about me. For some reason, the thought made my pulse race.

I stopped for a moment, having sped through the text up

to that point.

The thought made my pulse race.

I wondered, given the context, whether this was a sign that the author was male. Or was it possible that someone who'd had nothing that could be considered proper relationships with other people might become nervous, or find their heart racing, when meeting someone of the same sex? Was the author purposefully trying to obscure his or her gender? Or was that just me making assumptions as I read the text? I felt an impatient urge to read more, but this had the reverse effect of making me feel stupefied and absent-minded. I rested my elbows on the window frame and shifted my gaze outdoors.

Is this girl, Mitsuko, going to be the next one to die?

The window afforded a partial view of the road between our house and the one opposite, and as I watched, someone was walking down that narrow bit of road, folding up an umbrella. I stood bolt upright. I couldn't be totally sure, but it looked like Dad.

There wasn't any time to think. I gathered the scattered notebooks and slid them back into the manila envelope. I put the envelope into the cardboard box, then pushed the handbag with the bundle of hair still inside and shoved the old clothes haphazardly on top. I shut the closet, closed the study door, and launched myself down the stairs. When I got to the kitchen I could already hear the jangle of keys in the front door.

"Ah, I thought something was off. The door was already unlocked," Dad said, looking up at me as he pulled the door open.

"Yeah, sorry, welcome back. No one wants to bring their dog in when the weather's like this and I had nothing else to do, so I figured I'd stop by." I wiped the sweat from my forehead, trying to make it look like I was brushing away my hair. Something in me had changed definitively since I'd walked into the house a mere hour earlier. But I had to make sure Dad didn't notice. "Is it still raining?"

"It's not that bad, the wind's the problem. You been here long?"

"Around fifteen minutes. I was lying down in the living room, just about to doze off." We walked into the kitchen and I opened the fridge. "Want a drink?"

"A beer would be nice."

I pulled out two cans and handed one to Dad, who was sitting down. "How do you feel?"

"Quit asking that every time. I'm just the same as before—nothing wrong in particular, except that I can't get to sleep."

I felt a sudden burning thirst as soon as I lifted the can to my mouth, and almost drained the whole thing in one gulp while still on my feet.

I had just wiped my hand over my mouth when Dad looked at me. "Well, take a load off."

"Sure." Sitting with him before me, I suddenly felt anxious about not being able to recall the kinds of things we usually discussed. The atmosphere was heavy. In any case, I thought it would seem odd if I didn't ask why he had been out. "So where were you?"

"Just pachinko. I was up, then pushed my luck and lost it all."

"Pachinko? But…why…" In all the years I'd known Dad, I had never once heard of him going to play pachinko. I couldn't picture him sitting there, patient among the noise and the throngs of people.

"What? I'm not averse to a bit of pachinko. The place behind the station, 'New Eden,' pays out pretty good when you win. Say, if the shop doesn't need you, will you stay for some food?"

"Ah, I was actually thinking I should go to the dentist. I've had a toothache for a while, kept putting it off and now it's really starting to kill me. I haven't made an appointment so I guess I'll have to wait there for a while, but I'd hate it to get any worse overnight. I'll swing by another time for dinner."

Even I thought it sounded like a shoddy excuse, but Dad just nodded and said, "I see." He suggested I take an umbrella so I grabbed a random one from the stand on my way out.

I looked at my watch and saw that it was 4:30. I rushed towards the station, putting in a call to my brother Yohei on the way. I used the lure of a steak dinner to convince him to meet me outside Kyoto Station at six. He was a university student and rented an apartment in the city. I called work next and when Ms. Hosoya answered I explained that something had come up; I told her I wouldn't be back before closing and asked if everything was okay. Now that Chie was gone, Ms. Hosoya was the only full-time staff. She was middle-aged and soft-spoken, yet very capable, and I had a tendency to always ask a little too much of her.

"With weather like this there aren't any dogs out in the field. We've got people at four tables inside. It's quiet, the dogs are all well-behaved, so not much barking. And we just had two new members join."

As this meant cash, a part of me that had become brutal was slightly mollified. With business as it was, even a single change in membership had a significant effect.

"That's good to hear, especially as we just lost someone."

"They were moving away, remember, there was nothing we could have done about that."

"What kind of dogs do they have? The new members."

"One is an elderly Beagle, the other's a large Bernese Mountain Dog."

I couldn't help grinning. I almost asked which was bigger, Cujo or the new dog. The week before, Ms. Hosoya had been crouched down in the field when a male Bernese named Cujo knocked her over. For a good ten seconds, everyone, including myself, had just stood dumbstruck and watched. She struggled wordlessly on the ground as the dog slobbered its heavy, oversized tongue over her face and glasses until the owner rushed from the bathroom and pulled the dog away.

She had been pale when I helped her to her feet. As her arms went frantically around my neck, the momentum carried her forward and her lips pressed against my cheek. To make matters worse, some of the buttons on her blouse had come undone, giving me a clear view of her white bra. The skin of her chest was alluring, nearly as white as her bra, and for a moment I felt a brief thrill while the fact that she was as old as my late mother blinked out of my mind.

She didn't emerge from the bathroom for a long while after that.

She was regularly overworked and her pay was modest,

so I worried she might use the occasion as an excuse to quit. Luckily she had chosen to stay on, but it became taboo to mention the subject at work. The following day Nachi, a part-timer, brought in a particular book by Stephen King, thinking it a kindness, and said he would lend it to her. I confiscated it on the spot. I was constantly finding myself surprised by his actions, and to top that off, just a few days later I discovered he'd snapped a photo with his phone of Ms. Hosoya trapped beneath the dog. I only found this out because he'd shown it to me, practically boasting about it.

"Did you laugh just now, boss?" She caught me off guard, sounding like she could see right through me from the other end of the line.

"No, I…"

"Anyway, the new members. I charged double the enrollment and membership fees for the Bernese. Those large dogs can be dangerous, as I'm sure you know. I think we should make this a new policy from now on."

"Ah, but, uhm… I think, first we should…"

There was an awkward pause. Then she calmly added, "Just kidding."

4

"If it was me I'd ask, before getting upset over it. I'd just tell him I found some notebooks and ask what they were," Yohei said, washing down a mouthful of food with a swig of beer.

In all but an emergency, my kid brother would drop whatever he was doing and travel anywhere, at any time of day, for a free steak. He would order it bloody rare and devour it like a dog.

"You could try to savor that a little more, since I'm spending so much on this meal."

"Yeah right, this place is barely a step up from a diner. This meat wouldn't go down if I tried to enjoy it."

Every now and then I felt like I wanted to throw Yohei into the dog run to let him run around with the other mutts for a day. Knowing him, he'd climb through the ranks and become their leader, then try to rape one of the female bulldogs.

I had relayed the story in as much detail as possible, but Yohei hadn't been taking it seriously. If anything, he looked clearly incredulous. I supposed that as he hadn't actually read the notebooks, it was perhaps unavoidable that it didn't sink in immediately.

"Look, Ryo, I'm not saying I won't help out if you insist.

But I'm pretty sure you'll find it's nothing at all if you read to the end." Yohei nodded at me, making it seem like he was the older brother and not the other way around.

I had chosen to confide in my cheeky kid brother because, if I wanted to keep reading the notebooks without Dad finding out, I had no other choice than to work with an accomplice I could trust.

I had a plan. Every Sunday evening, without fail, Dad went to visit Gran at her nursing home near Yamato Koriyama. I had to use that opportunity to sneak into the house and continue reading. Yohei would meet up with Dad and delay him as much as possible. Then, when they parted ways at the train station on the way home, Yohei would phone me. That was all I needed.

The next Sunday was in two days. It was the busiest day for the cafe, and as the field got crowded the dogs had a tendency to fight. But now wasn't the time to be worrying about that. And Yohei happened to have time on his hands that day, so I decided to move the plan into action.

"Sorry to get you involved in this weirdness at a time like this," I said, avoiding looking at his face.

"No problem, we'll just play it like we always do."

I think he was trying to act cool, but his tone was stilted, which made him sound a little angry. When Mom died Yohei had cried his eyes out, and ever since he made a point of never saying anything even vaguely sad in front of me. Even when it came to Dad's condition we had developed an unspoken rule between us: we would pretend it didn't exist. It was the best we could do in the absence of any practical way to help, and there was also the childish hope that ignoring the illness might bring about a miracle. While we would sometimes come apart at the seams, we always made sure to act carefree and smile when we ate steak together.

"I need to find out who wrote them, at least. It's got to be either Mom or Dad, though, based on where I found them."

"What about the penmanship?"

"Hmm, it wasn't like either of theirs. The characters were uneven, like a grade school kid's."

"Hmm."

Having finished eating, Yohei started to eye my plate, so I cut him a big portion of my steak even though I'd eaten less than half. I started to eat faster so he wouldn't pinch any more.

"You think it's Dad, don't you. You're wondering if he's actually a psychotic serial killer, if he murdered your real mother before she was substituted with someone else or whatever? Whoa, dude, that's scary."

"No, that's not what I..." I gulped down some of the now-flat beer in an attempt to hide the fact that I couldn't deny it outright. Truth be told, those exact thoughts had flitted in and out of my mind the whole time I had been reading the notebooks. I'd even had the absurd suspicion pop into my mind that Dad had been the real cause of Mom's crosswalk accident two months earlier. And the childhood memory that my mother had been replaced felt increasingly real, lodged in my gut ever since it first came back to me. I had even considered the possibility that Dad had killed both my first and second mothers with his own hands.

"Come to think of it, there was something strange about the way Granddad died. If what you're saying is right, Ryo, maybe that was Dad's doing, too..."

The measured timing of the odd remark made my mind go momentarily blank. It felt like some bizarre darkness was trying to swallow me whole.

Granddad had passed away when I was still in my freshman year of high school. It had happened without warning. The doctors said it was acute heart failure, even though he had no chronic illness. He had been dozing under a *kotatsu* warmer and had already stopped breathing when Dad tried to wake him. It was a Sunday, and Dad had been the only other person in the house. Mom and Gran had taken Yohei and myself out shopping when it happened.

"Oh? Come on, don't get angry. Sorry, that was shitty, even for a joke," Yohei, stunned at my sudden pallor, offered a genuine apology, then tried a subtle change of subject. "Think about it though, this theory you have of Mom being replaced by someone else—that makes us half-brothers." He winked, jabbing his fork in my direction. "That's kind of cool, you know, dramatic, or something."

I had, of course, already thought about this. With him sitting in front of me it was hard to imagine it was true, but I wasn't ready to joke about it either.

I hadn't taken after either of my parents, but Yohei's eyes and facial features had clearly come from Mom. They also shared a number of traits beyond their looks—slight far-sightedness, dog- and cat-hair allergies. It felt stupid, but those kind of things had begun to weigh on my mind.

"Let me ask you then. Who else could have written it if it wasn't Dad? Don't tell me you think it was Mom."

"Why not? She could totally have written such stuff."

I was stunned into silence.

"She could have written it when she was young, maybe she wanted to submit it to some magazine. She loved books, and she used to read loads of novels... Y'know, she had that daydreamer side to her, and she was quite the romantic."

Daydreamer? Romantic? Was it possible that, as younger and elder sons, we had wildly different impressions of Mom? She used to bring books home from the library, I knew that, but she was plain and mild-mannered, the very model of a housewife. There was no way I could believe a love of books made her a romantic, much less the kind of person to do something like write a novel.

I wanted to push Yohei on the subject, but he'd turned his face down while he was talking about Mom and now he was blinking rapidly. The steak was gone. I looked away and mumbled something vague.

"Hey, calling Mom a bit of a daydreamer made me re-member this weird thing," he said, keeping his voice flat to mask the embarrassment of me seeing him with damp eyes.

"What is it?"

"Never mind."

"Hey, come on, stop acting like a brat. You've already started to say something, so out with it."

"It's just... I don't like it when you twist my words, Ryo. You already have."

I was well aware of how antagonistic he could get if I was too direct, so I retrieved a menu and made him choose something for dessert in the hope that we might start again. Once we placed our orders I put the question to him, trying to sound casual. "Hey, Yohei, did Mom seem a little strange to you towards the end?"

"Strange? In what way?" His voice was tight when he threw the question back at me. He'd probably noticed something odd about her behavior, too.

I said nothing and waited.

"I suppose, now that you mention it, she did seem a little gloomy. Like bursting into tears in the middle of watching TV. And she'd give a jolt, sometimes, when I called to her."

"Do you think she…"

"She what?"

"Was she scared of something?"

"Like what?"

"Ah, I really don't know, but… Say for example she found the notebooks and read them."

"And back to the notebooks! Why do you keep bringing them up? What, you're saying she read them, found out her husband was a murderer, and got freaked out?"

"You can't say that that's a hundred percent impossible, can you?"

"There's something wrong with you, Ryo. Of course she was afraid. She knew Dad was going to…pass away soon. It would've been weird if she hadn't been afraid."

I found myself with nothing to say in response. He was exactly right. Not to mention, that was probably what I had thought at the time. If I had let something like that slip from my mind, I was forced to wonder if there was something drastically wrong in the way I was looking at things. Perhaps it was all some kind of wild delusion I'd cooked up.

"You're right, I'm sorry." It was my turn to apologize. And yet I couldn't help thinking back to Mom, stooped forwards as she dragged her feet in Dad's sandals; there had been an entirely different type of fear in her eyes that day, something that hinted at a much more sordid secret. "Yohei, what was it you were about to say just now about Mom? Spit it out."

"But it's from way back, it doesn't matter now."

"Whatever, just say it."

"Well, when Granddad was still alive we used to share a room, right? There was this one time, I think you were still in seventh grade, when I woke up in the middle of the night. I opened my eyes a bit and saw Mom sitting by your bed, watching your face."

"And?"

"Yeah, well. She kind of… She was holding a pillow to her chest."

"…"

"Ah, see? You're twisting it already, that's why I didn't want to say anything. It wasn't like she was—"

"Oh, you mean she wasn't about to smother me with a pillow?"

"Of course she wasn't, don't be stupid. Anyways, I pretended I was asleep, wondering what she was watching you for, and after a while she just got up and walked out. I remember thinking it was weird as I went back to sleep. See, I only just remembered that when you said that stuff about Mom being switched with someone else."

"What was she holding the pillow for?"

"I don't know, she was probably half-asleep."

"Hey, doesn't our family seem a little weird, the more you think about it?"

"How so?"

"Well, for example, Mom and Dad never tried to mix with other people." My parents were decidedly antisocial. Even with the neighbors they hardly ventured beyond basic greetings.

"That's just because they got along well and preferred each other's company."

I remembered something the moment Yohei said this. The fact that I could recall such a trivial thing seemed to suggest it had stuck in my mind, that it didn't quite make sense. "What about when Dad bought that microscope? That was middle school too, right?"

It had been a Sunday. Dad had taken us to the Takashimaya department store in Namba. We were in the middle of eating lunch in the food court when a man we'd never seen before came over. Dad sprang to his feet. I worked out from their conversation that the man had been a colleague of Dad's from his old job in Tokyo. The man animatedly explained that he had left that job, too, a few years earlier to take over the family business; that he was from Osaka originally and was out visiting clients even though it was a Sunday. When they said goodbye the man suggested they get together for a drink sometime soon and offered Dad his business card. When Dad said he had forgotten to bring his, the man pulled out an address book and copied down the name and number of Dad's workplace. Yohei and I looked at each other—Dad had given the man a completely fictitious name, and probably a made-up number, too. To make things worse, when he'd paid for the microscope, I had happened to see him pull his cardholder from his inside pocket along with his wallet, while Yohei busily grinned and pawed at the top of the box.

When the man was gone, Yohei innocently asked Dad why he'd told the man a lie. Even then I knew it was probably better not to ask.

A long time ago he stole money from the company, he's a bad person, it's better we keep our distance. That was Dad's response. There was sweat on his forehead. I remembered being suddenly seized by a bizarre worry that it was in fact Dad and not the other man who had embezzled from the company. In hindsight, it was obvious Dad would never have done such a thing. He had always been light on worldly desires.

But Yohei didn't seem to remember it at all. "When he bought the microscope from Takashimaya? I can recall that day pretty clearly, you know. You sure you're not getting that memory mixed up with something else? Or maybe it's some hodgepodge of fantasy and memory."

"Don't talk nonsense."

"I mean, sure, Mom and Dad might have been a little insular, but come on, they were honest, upstanding citizens otherwise."

"All right, what about this. Don't normal parents like to tell their kids about when they were young, about their own childhoods? We hardly know a thing, only that Dad lost his parents when he was a kid. They never told us about how they met, what their lives were like before they were a couple. Plus, they never told us about when we were babies. It was like they purposefully avoided bringing up the past. Something happened back then, I'm sure of it."

"But Mom told me all about the time I was born. They were worried because I only weighed a little over five pounds. And I had downy hair, with fine black strands even on my back."

Yohei couldn't possibly know how much of a shock it was for me to hear that. "Mom told you all that?"

"Yeah."

I watched him as he dug into his pear pie and felt a lonely chill spread through my bosom. "I bet that was when I wasn't around. It fits, since you were born after the move to Komagawa. She wouldn't have said anything if I was there. If she told you about the time you were born, she'd have to do the same for me. I don't remember her ever telling me where I was born or what the experience was like. And all the photos, right? You know, they all got burned up years before in that fire, so not a single one was left."

"I don't really get it, but... You really, truly believe it, don't you? That Mom was switched with someone else when we moved to Komagawa."

For the first time Yohei looked bewildered. Or maybe his expression was closer to fear. I couldn't tell whether he was scared because he had started to doubt Mom and Dad, or whether he was simply scared of me.

5

The next day was a Saturday. There was a cool breeze and a light covering of clouds. Shaggy Head was fairly bustling, in the dog run and inside, and yet I was finding it impossible to concentrate on work. I was getting orders mixed up and taking out cakes without a fork. At one point I tripped over a leash and almost crushed a Chihuahua underfoot. I realized that Ms. Hosoya was watching me with a frown. It was before two p.m. and the day was still long.

Ms. Hosoya came over and asked, "What's up with you today, boss?"

"I didn't sleep much, I think I'm a little spaced out." It was true that I had hardly slept—I'd spent most of the night lost in thought.

"You're really pale, maybe you should go upstairs and lie down for a bit. The three of us can manage things down here."

One of the three was in the kitchen, meaning that without me Ms. Hosoya and Nachi would have to manage the floor, the run, and the register. That would be difficult.

"But I'm already causing enough trouble, what with me taking off early tomorrow." I had explained earlier in the morning that I would have to head out Sunday afternoon. I had managed to convince another member of the part-time staff to come in on her day off, but I felt bad regardless. "And Nachi is, well, he's like that." I nodded towards a table in the corner.

Whenever Clutch, a black pug, came to the cafe, Nachi never failed to come up with an excuse to neglect his work and fuss over the dog. He was already crouched next to the tiny creature, which was as small as a rat, stroking it with his index finger.

According to the elderly lady that owned him Clutch had an exceedingly noble pedigree, and that may have been why he was so small. "He's stayed a pup his whole life, even as he became an old man." He couldn't walk or bark, so the only thing to do was hold him gently, like something fragile. For some reason the odd creature, unrecognizable as a dog unless someone told you, appeared to be an endless source of happiness for Nachi.

Ms. Hosoya glared at his hunched back, clearly on the verge of tutting with disapproval. Nachi looked around, perhaps sensing her menacing mood, jumped to his feet, and walked over with a sheepish grin.

"Ha ha. I wish he'd chew on my finger, just one time." Nachi always said this. The tiny dog was incapable of moving anything beyond its eyes and mouth, so gnawing at a finger was the only way for the small creature to express affection. But Clutch only ever bit his owner. "When he bites her, she says it's so sweet and cute that she could cry."

"Yes, well, as you can see Nachi here will do his best to help, so go and get a little rest. You're only bringing down the mood, looking that sickly. Go on, off you go." She shooed me upstairs, waving me off like I was a dog.

"Thank you, maybe just an hour, then."

I padded up the stairs, still in my apron. For some reason I walked as softly as I could.

The second floor, consisting of a couple of small rooms, a kitchenette, and a bathroom like the kind found in business hotels, was where I lived. The plate and mug I'd used for breakfast were still on the table, but I couldn't summon the energy to clean up.

I went over to the window and stood there for a while, watching the field through the thin curtains. As it was a quarter of an acre in size, it was a little too cramped for the larger dogs to dash about freely. Even so, these days facilities such as these were the only places dogs could run around outside without a leash.

Some of the dogs seemed lonesome, wagging their tails at their owners watching from the veranda, while others darted back and forth in endless drifting circles.

At its northern edge the field lifted into a gradual slope which stretched out beyond the fence, connecting with a wood at the foothills of a small mountain.

I could see Chie at the fence, working with a shovel. Long, slender limbs. She wore gloves and had a towel tucked around her neck as she filled in the various holes made by the dogs—

Memories of her dwelt on the grounds and in my room like ghosts, frightening me.

We had once gone past the fence a little ways into the woods and made love in broad daylight, on an overhang above a mountain stream that served as a natural observation platform. While we were anxious of hikers happening upon us we let the strange lust take hold of us anyway. In the end we only accomplished half of what we desired and rushed back to my room. For the next three days—the whole of the last August's *O-bon* holiday—we gave up on plans to see movies or go on drives and instead shut ourselves up in my room, barely leaving my creaky single bed.

When I heard Chie was gone, it was purely a physical sensation of loss that hit me first. It was so powerful that it knocked the life out of me, and it took a while before I was able to register the sadness in my heart. I still didn't know, even today, if it was Chie herself that I missed, or if it was her smell, her warmth, her weight, the touch of her skin, the physical sensation of her.

She had been dressed in the light clothes of a hiker when she turned up unexpectedly at the construction site a couple of years ago, just as we were finishing up work on the cafe's foundations. She had been walking the hills when she had caught sight of the "Opening Soon" sign at the worksite entrance, and apparently had known immediately that she wanted to work at the cafe.

When she took off her cap her face was pale and radiant in the light, gleaming with a light sheen of sweat. She had a mysterious power over me from the beginning.

She had graduated from a vocational college in Okayama before starting work at a trading company in Osaka. After that she went through a number of jobs, never finding anything she genuinely enjoyed. She was strong for a woman and madly in love with dogs, perfect for a place like Shaggy Head. She said she wouldn't be fussy about pay if I took her on.

As she told me this, her willful expression occasionally

slipped into something altogether more fragile, and for some reason the strange contrast roiled my emotions. I kept getting so worked up that I had to look away.

I was in a daze thinking about her for the rest of the day, right until I got into bed that night. Even though we had only spoken briefly, I couldn't bear the thought that the woman called Chie had expressions that I had not yet seen. I had to see them all for myself. I was surprised to realize that I would do whatever was necessary to make that happen.

The busy months that led up to the cafe opening were like a happy dream. Chie was perfect for the job, and I had already suspected that a woman's perspective would be necessary for running a business of this kind. She happily threw herself into helping, displaying her own unique style as she worked on the interior of the cafe, on plans for the kitchen equipment, and even on the design of the cafe's logo. It was her idea to plant flowering ash trees between the parking lot and the building, and her choice to have thick, cement-colored cups and saucers.

As we worked to get the cafe ready for opening, our personal relationship rapidly developed. I had already stopped thinking of Shaggy Head as my business—in my head, the cafe was ours. We discussed starting dog-training classes, opening a "hotel" to board pets on a short-term basis, doing more thorough testing to find the best coffee beans, and baking additive-free bread. Our future seemed to naturally unfold before us.

Once the business was running smoothly we would buy a house in a nearby residential area, and we didn't care if it was old or small. We would build a wooden deck around it, plant flowers in the garden, and raise kids in a stress-free environment. We talked about these things as though they were all long since decided.

It all felt so natural I hardly felt the need to propose. When I gave her a ring, a year later, it was purely out of a sense of formality.

Then she disappeared. It was almost half a year ago, in early February.

Blustery winds bearing sleet had all but shut down the cafe for a few days. I didn't pay much attention when Chie didn't come in. She had left early the day before, looking unwell and saying she might take the next day off. She didn't answer when I phoned, so I assumed she was asleep and decided not to bother her with any more calls. After closing up that night I bought some groceries, *udon* noodles and scallions and things, and went to check on her. She lived in a small studio apartment a couple of minutes' walk from the train stop at Nabata.

The windows were pitch black and she didn't answer when I knocked on the door as usual. It didn't worry me, as I still thought she was probably just asleep.

I'll never forget the way that feeling slammed into me, of everything collapsing around me, when I used the spare key to open the door.

The room was totally vacant. The familiar curtains were gone, as were the bed, table, and cutlery. The thin veil of darkness seemed to insinuate that the room had always been that way.

I kicked off my shoes and stumbled a few steps inside. I wonder how long I sat crumpled and dazed in the middle of the floor that had been laid bare from corner to corner. I couldn't process any of it but the question looped through my mind all the same, like something mechanical: *What's going on? What the hell is going on? What's going on? What the hell is going on?*

I searched for over a month, neglecting work completely. I tried the real estate agent that managed the room, but they didn't have her new address. All they told me was that she had paid the early termination fee in full before moving out. I went back to the studio apartment block a number of times, speaking to her neighbors on either side first, then to everyone else in the building, but I didn't gain any useful information. I couldn't even find a single person who had shared more than polite greetings with her.

Time and again I went back to bars and pubs we had visited together. As I sat there drinking alone I was unable to stop myself from turning around and checking the door as though she might just waltz in at any moment with an impish grin on her face.

That was when it dawned on me that when it came to specifics, I knew next to nothing about her. Our conversations had always focused on the future of Shaggy Head, what our future selves would be like. I had been blind when it came to anything else.

I knew she was an only child, and I knew her parents lived in Okayama as we had been talking about going there so she could introduce me, but she never told me their actual address. I had no idea about the kind of relationships she'd had before, what her friends were like, the details of her old jobs, or what she liked to do when she was alone.

Just a couple of weeks before she disappeared, I'd agreed to loan her some money after she'd begged me: two million yen, the whole of my savings. Chie had told me that her cousin had embezzled ten million yen from her workplace and that she was now facing criminal charges unless she could scrape enough together from friends and relatives and return it in full.

Ms. Hosoya had seemed distressed, too. She had called the college listed on Chie's resume, even the local ward office for anything that might have listed a new address. The college turned out to be real, but they wouldn't release alumni names to unrelated parties, and the ward office refused to let anyone but the person in question examine records. Ms. Hosoya grew more and more despondent, as she had doted on Chie like a daughter. I think she might have suspected Chie of making off with the money, of having approached me in the first place for such a purpose. It was understandable, considering how things had unfolded.

But I couldn't believe it. That wasn't the sort of woman Chie was. I still didn't believe it, and even if I never saw her again I probably wouldn't until the day I die. After having held her trembling body in my arms so many times, my body continued to scream that it was absolutely impossible.

I dragged myself away from the window. I had to make a conscious effort just to move. I sat at my desk but my head was still heavy so I rested it in my hands. I tried to force my thoughts away from Chie.

Without any particular reason I narrowed my eyes a little and looked at the sheets of paper scattered across the surface of the desk: copies of my family register, current and old. Supplementary family registers. Residency certificates.

I had made a trip to the library before opening the cafe that morning, remembering it housed a ward office branch that was open for basic service on weekends. I realized they would probably have information on my parents' old address in Tokyo. I wasn't sure what I would do even if I had been able to pin down the twenty-year-old address. Would I go to Tokyo looking for their old neighbors, hold up a photo of Mom, and ask if it was the same person? I think a part of me was considering trying that much at least. I didn't care what, I just wanted to know something of my family's past.

Either way, the address had proved elusive. What little information there was told me I was born in Tokyo's Kita Ward, but even then the name of the hospital was missing.

I had already known that our address in Komagawa was listed as our current permanent residence. The transfer had been processed during the move. When I checked in the official copy of the register, the relocation to Komagawa in Nara Prefecture was recorded as being from Maebashi in Gunma Prefecture. Maebashi was Mom's old house where my grandparents had lived, so there wasn't anything particularly strange in that.

I was surprised, however, to find the Maebashi address also listed as the old address on the residency certificate and slips. They'd been living in Tokyo, so why was the Tokyo address not listed?

At first a number of theories crowded my head. I was suddenly sure of a cover-up, of their doctoring the forms to keep the Tokyo address a secret. Then I remembered the fire.

After that they had left the apartment in Tokyo and moved in temporarily with Mom's parents, so it was possible they listed their residency there at the time. At least the parts fit, if that was the case.

I was still intent on finding out the Tokyo address, our home before Maebashi. Later in the morning I did some more research online and found out that the Maebashi City Hall had a "Notice of Removal" form that was issued when the family register was moved to Komagawa. If I checked it out, there was a chance I could work out the old address. I was excited, and if it hadn't been for the fact that it was a Saturday I would probably have gone straight to Maebashi.

As things were, there was nothing I could do.

If it wasn't for her condition, I could have gone to the nursing home and dropped it into conversation with Gran. Her dementia, however, had gotten so bad she no longer remembered that her daughter, my mother, was dead. The worst thing for me was the fact that my own memory was proving useless. No matter how hard I tried, I couldn't remember a thing from before my hospitalization. Not the house I lived in, not its surroundings, not a single thing. The first memories of my childhood were all from inside the hospital. They were scattered but vivid: the other kids in the ward, the kind nurses, the toy robot Dad brought for me.

No records, no memories, just a handful of bizarre notebooks...

With my chin still resting in one hand I picked up the family register. I looked back at the ruthless and business-like line that had been struck diagonally through the name Misako, my mother's name. It was painful to see such a stark reminder of the fact of her death, and yet I couldn't help thinking of what Yohei had said. She had watched me sleeping with a pillow clutched to her chest. I couldn't find it in my heart to grieve for her death anymore, not properly.

Whenever I brought her familiar image that I'd absorbed throughout the years to mind, it was overlaid by another, an image of a young woman in a flowery dress, like a double exposure photograph. Short, wavy hair. Pale arms. One arm held that handbag, and she had a folded parasol in her hand. While I could tell she was smiling, her face was hazy: blank, whitish, with no eyes or mouth but looking at me and smiling regardless. At the bottom of my memories undulated a lapping fusion of sadness and fear.

Had someone really switched with Mom? If so, what had happened to the woman who was my mother until I was four?

My mind raced in circles, always coming back to these same questions. I let out a sigh. I'd been sighing all day.

I wondered if I was somehow intent on convincing myself it was all true: the contents of the notebooks, the memory of someone replacing Mom. With my mother dead from a car accident, Chie gone, Dad ill and getting weaker, Gran with dementia, and my business teetering on the brink of collapse, maybe all I wanted to do was lose myself in the fantasy and escape the reality around me.

One of the dogs had started barking outside. They usually just ran around, so it was rare that they made much noise. I checked the clock and saw it was almost four. I stood up in shock. I had come up saying I'd only take an hour, but I was already long past that.

Halfway down the stairs, I heard more barking and began to worry. Trouble between the dogs had to be settled before it got out of hand and became a real problem. One time, the hysteria had spread to all the dogs in the field and it had almost reached the point of bloodshed. The excitement had been quick to die down and the dogs went back to being their usual selves, but it had been a different story for the owners. They started to criticize each other for not disciplining their animals properly, and a number wouldn't let the issue go. A few even cancelled their memberships over it.

When I got to the field, however, I found that nothing was amiss. The barking was just a pair of Miniature Schnauzers pestering their owner to throw a ball for them to fetch. The sun was still high with interspersed clouds that were dazzlingly white.

Nachi was off to one side, trying to get a Shiba to run through a thick tube we'd put there as a plaything. The dog's owner stood next to them, a woman and quite a looker. I supposed Nachi had said goodbye to Clutch for the day.

The Shiba was frightened to go into the wide bit of collapsible tubing, but Nachi was already an old hand at this—he was part-time staff but had worked at the cafe from the beginning. The dog kept glancing up at him looking for a chance to escape, but Nachi's quiet assertiveness eventually tamed him.

Watching the scene I felt a breeze blow softly through my over-heated head. Ms. Hosoya walked over with perfect timing, placing a coffee on the empty table beside me. I took a grateful sip as the Shiba disappeared again into the tubing, spurred on by the taste of his initial success and followed this time by a succession of dogs, their curiosity piqued.

The customers with drinks on the tables on the veranda seemed to be enjoying the show, and the pretty owner of the Shiba looked impressed as she thanked Nachi. He replied that it was nothing, pulling a quick salute-like gesture. It seemed clear that she and most of the other customers thought Nachi, with his big frame and even bigger attitude, was the proprietor of Shaggy Head, and to my exasperation he showed no signs of wanting to correct anyone on this.

A large Retriever ran into the tube, causing the whole thing to wriggle like a worm. One of the customers joked that it was probably stuck, causing everyone to burst out laughing. Most of the other dogs were ambling around the field, looking content with whatever toy they'd been given. They seemed human somehow, perhaps because they looked a bit pathetic.

Yet everything felt great as it was. To me, the closed-in space full of dogs was a strange kind of utopia. I was certain that if I waited here long enough Chie would come back.

6

I kept watch from the second-floor window of a coffee shop by the train station, waiting for Dad to show. The area was bustling so I was afraid I might miss him, but at around half past three I caught sight of him in a moss-green polo shirt he often wore. He was making his way towards the station, his back straight, but with less vigor than usual. It seemed demonstrative of his worsening condition. Visiting hours weren't particularly fixed, but Dad always aimed to get there by five so he could help feed Gran dinner.

I waited until I was sure he was definitely past the ticket gates before leaving the coffee shop. As I hurried down the road to the house, I kept thinking remorsefully that it still wasn't too late to turn back. I knew that reading the notebooks to the end could cause irreparable harm. Yet the magnetic allure was still there, in direct conflict with my reservations, powerful enough to physically spur me on.

Entering through the front door I went directly upstairs and into Dad's study, without even pausing to put my hands together before Mom's photograph. The air smelled of cigarettes, so I guessed he'd been smoking there until he went out. When I opened the closet door, everything looked to be just as I'd left it after rushing to put the boxes back a couple of days earlier. I felt weak with relief.

I pulled out and held the white handbag before retrieving the manila envelope from the bottom of the box. The moment I caught a whiff of the dusty leather I saw the image of the ghost-like woman. The woman wearing the flower-print dress, smiling at me. It was possible she was my mother. My real mother, but probably long dead.

I didn't know what to think about her.

I breathed out, in, out again. I had to stop wasting time.

I carried the envelope to the window where it was brighter, then took the notebooks out. I chose the one marked with the number two and thumbed quickly through it. I suddenly couldn't remember how much I'd read, but then I saw the name Mitsuko.

Oh, right. The protagonist had dissuaded Mitsuko from stealing, and they had been about to leave the store together.

The moment I started reading I almost dropped the notebook.

The narrator, the author was a woman!

It was right there in the text, as plain as day. I couldn't pull my eyes from the passage that described what the protagonist was wearing. It no longer made sense that this was something Dad had written, that it was his diary...

All the thoughts I'd put together shattered into pieces. I leaned against the window for a while, my mind blank. I only came back to myself when my phone chimed with a text alert. It was Yohei: *Bumped into Dad at Yamato Koriyama, leaving to see Gran now.* I typed "OK" in response, my fingers almost comically shaky.

If the notebooks weren't a diary it was possible it was a

work of fiction, something Dad had written from the perspective of a female character. But no, I still didn't believe it was made up. I couldn't shake the gut feeling that, whatever the story was, it was real.

It had to be someone's diary. A confession. And if that someone wasn't Dad, the only alternative was Mom. Who else could it be?

Still shaken, I started to devour the text.

"Just that? Come on, then. This one's on me."

There was an apathetic youth manning the register, and I suspected he would have turned a blind eye even if he had caught her shoplifting.

I hadn't really been interested in her before, but I had for a while felt that Mitsuko and I were something like kindred spirits. I wondered if the theatrical, mask-like coating of makeup she wore was the flip side of whatever force it was that compelled me to remain hidden. The familiarity she had just displayed might, I mused, be because she sensed the same about me. For some reason, the thought made my pulse race.

We were walking down the street, side by side after leaving the store, when Mitsuko ripped open the bag of popcorn she had just bought and plunged her hand in and started to munch away.

"Want some?"

She held the bag out, so I took a little. We walked a little more, reaching the fountain in front of the art museum.

"Want to sit?" Mitsuko asked another question, and we found a bench to sit on. Without warning, she reached over and flicked away some popcorn that was stuck to my top.

"The frills on your blouse are really cute. Where did you get it?" she asked, but went to throw the empty bag into the bin nearby instead of paying attention to my answer. When she got back she pulled open another bag of candy and began to eat them at a leisurely pace. She held the bag out to me with a questioning hum. "So, got any plans for today?"

I didn't know how to respond to a question like that.

"What was your name? I forget."

I told her my name, then guessing it might seem strange to leave it at that, followed by asking the question that had been on my mind the whole time. "What happened to your hand?"

"Oh, this?" She brought her left wrist to her face and examined the bandage where some blood had seeped through. "This was yesterday. I cut myself again."

I didn't say anything, as I didn't quite follow her meaning. No one talked about cutting back then—I think the trend was yet to set in, or maybe I was just unaware of it.

Mitsuko poked out her chin, unimpressed with my ignorance. She started to explain wrist-cutting to me, her voice pitched high, child-like. Her makeup was so thick I couldn't imagine what she'd look like without it. She didn't look human, it was like an android or something was talking at me.

She told me she'd first tried it because it was trendy in America. She said she'd kept it up because it made her feel fashionable, because the bandages were cool, and because the bleeding helped clear her head. And before she realized, she was addicted.

When she finished talking she jumped to her feet and brushed some candy crumbs from her knees, then said "See ya!" and hurried out of sight.

After that, whenever we saw each other at school Mitsuko

would come over and say hi, sometimes wrapping her arm around mine. We bumped into each other a lot, so I had to assume she was seeking me out on purpose.

After the third or so invitation, I visited her apartment. It was obvious from the room that she had no problems with money, so I figured she probably had a decent allowance coming in. Everything in the room, from the cushions to the curtains and wall hangings all bore a profusion of flower prints, frills, lamé, and beading, and her cosmetics alone could fill up a clothes trunk. The room was full with the heavy tang of perfume, old clothing, sweat, and blood. It was the first time I visited someone's room and, more importantly, it was the first time I chatted at length one on one.

I got the strong impression that it was the same for Mitsuko. We had become friends, it seemed, and yet neither of us really knew how one was supposed to handle a friend. She made some tea and we sat for something like half an hour. The whole time she was engrossed in eating popcorn and uncharacteristically laconic. We didn't do anything else that day, but when I was about to leave she presented me with a spare key.

"Hey, hey, so after you left I made a really deep cut," she said the next day, as if it was an afterthought, holding up her hand wrapped in thick bandages. "You'll come again today?"

On the way over I got her to wait while I picked up some dried *nori* seaweed and a few pounds of rice from the local supermarket. With the apparently unused rice cooker in her kitchen, I boiled the rice and rolled it into bite-sized chunks, each as big as half an egg, and wrapped them in thin strips of seaweed before telling Mitsuko to try them. Watching her eat nothing but candy made me feel terrible. She protested at first, saying anything other than candy would make her puke, but I paid no attention.

"I don't care if you throw up, just try them."

She ate the first of the rice balls with tears in her eyes, making it look like she was swallowing a caterpillar or something.

"Another," I said. Then another…and another. After the fifth she began to take a rice ball even when I said nothing, eventually eating about ten. Even after those, she occasionally took one of the rice balls still on the plate and put it in her mouth, as if suddenly noticing they were there. She told me various things about herself.

"I take these off when I'm at home," she said, peeling the bandages from her wrist and revealing the incisions to me for the first time. Brown stripes like those on the belly of a tabby cat lined the space between her wrist and the middle of her forearm. Some were old, others were still red and damp. A couple looked quite deep.

"Does it hurt when you cut yourself?"

"Of course it does. It'd be pretty dull if it didn't." When all the rice balls were gone Mitsuko opened a bag of caramel popcorn and tipped the contents onto the empty plate, then started to pick at that, too. "Sometimes there's hardly any blood, even when I make a deep cut. It makes me restless so I make even more cuts. Blood's warm, you know. It feels great when it runs together from a number of cuts and starts to trickle off my arm. I think I hit a vein once. It was amazing, there was so much blood, but I collapsed and passed out when I tried to wash the wound. I've been taking iron supplements since that time. I wonder why red, though. Not blue, not green. I think red's kind of special, more than the other colors. But the blood dries the moment it's outside. Like, look at the cover of this cushion. Turns into this horrible-looking stain."

I was quiet, listening to what she had to say, but she sounded like the narrator of some story, something from a video rented on a whim. The way she spoke didn't give me any real sense of how it felt to cut oneself.

The whole time, for some reason I was wondering whether there might be some way to stop Mitsuko from doing this. I didn't want to let her cut herself anymore, even though I knew she might someday die by my hand.

Strange men would sometimes call out to us when we were walking together outside. I suppose they regarded a woman who wore heavy makeup as someone that would readily sleep with anybody. For men, the fact that Mitsuko was an odd stick-like thing didn't bother them so long as they could have sex with her.

Among those men was a young worker at a ramen joint that was close to Mitsuko's apartment. We'd never been inside the place, but whenever he saw us, either on his way out or coming back from a delivery, he always tried to flirt with Mitsuko.

If she caught him watching, she gave a disgusted look. Yet, all of a sudden she'd start walking seductively nonetheless.

"Oh shit, it's Ramen again."

"Ladies, ladies. How 'bout a drive next time I'm off? I've got a pretty good set of wheels."

We'd taken to calling him Ramen; he had terrible skin and buckteeth, and from what we could tell he was essentially a walking ball of lust. He would bring his delivery moped to a stop and grin to show he'd had lots of experience with girls, but all the while his gaze would shift restlessly with fear.

"Ugh, no thanks," Mitsuko said, after we'd ignored him and walked on. "He's like a dog in heat. I bet he jerks off ten times a day."

"You do that yourself, Mitsuko." The words slipped from my mouth.

Her eyes went wide; it was hard to make out where her eyeliner ended and her eyelids began. "Eww. Don't be gross, I don't masturbate."

"Cutting's just a variation of getting yourself off."

I was still trying to get her to eat more, little by little, thinking she might lose interest in cutting herself if her diet improved. I had made potato salads, noodle dishes, and omelettes after the rice ball meal. I was making progress, but she still couldn't stop herself. There were fresh bloodstains on her bandages that day. I decided she might break the habit if I convinced her there was nothing cool about it, that it was as debased an action as touching herself.

At the same time, I became obsessed with thinking about how to end her life. It was on my mind whether I was with her or alone. When I imagined doing it, I would get so excited my skin sometimes broke out in goosebumps. The desire existed alongside the wish for Mitsuko to stop cutting herself, without any sense of contradiction.

I realize that was strange, in hindsight.

Being told she was essentially masturbating seemed to get to her. She didn't stop cutting herself; instead she became increasingly depressed, doing it less often but making what seemed to be deeper wounds when she did.

One day, an idea came to me while I was in her room.

"Hey, could you try cutting me?" I asked.

"You… What? Don't say such weird shit out of nowhere." The trembling in her voice told me she was deeply afraid.

"If you do it to me, it's not masturbation."

"I don't want to cut anyone else. I feel sick just thinking about it."

"Well, how about you show me the blades you always use.

There's nothing wrong with looking. Come on, go and get them."

Although Mitsuko typically acted high and mighty, she was a marionette if I gave forceful orders. I got her to line the blades and everything else she used on the surface of the table. Then I sat down and faced her.

"I want you to show me how you do it."

She picked up one of the blades and stared at it.

"Look, it's okay. Just do it like you normally would."

There were a number of cutting blades, sanitary pads, plastic bags, bandages, and tape lined up on the table. Mitsuko, a vacant look on her face, pushed her scar-covered left hand into a plastic bag, then positioned a blade held in her right hand over her left wrist. Her sad eyes never left mine even as I nodded and she jerked the blade quickly to one side, leaving behind a red line. The cut was shallow enough that there was no blood. The transparent bag clouded slightly from the warmth of her perspiration.

"That looks easy enough. Can I touch it?"

I brushed the tip of my index finger across the new incision, and also traced the browned welts of her older cuts.

"Perhaps I could try doing it for you. So we can see how that feels."

She didn't seem to have any particular objections so I held her wrist steady and drew another red line, parallel to the one she had just made. I had to hold back a rising thrill as I leaned in closer, seeing a dewy, transparent liquid in the base wound from below before the blood started to seep in.

I held out my left hand.

"I want you to cut me, to mark our friendship."

Mitsuko was motionless for something like three minutes, neither of us saying a thing. Then she bent forwards and swept over my arm. It was over in an instant, leaving a moment before the gentle ache of pain. We faced each other as we held out our arms, both cut now, so they were above the table. Thin lines of blood trickled downwards from each of the new incisions. My hope was that through cutting me, by cutting somebody else, Mitsuko's urges might change direction and move away from herself.

She jumped up like she'd snapped out of a daze, then dressed her arm with practiced speed before applying one of the pads to my wrist and finally wrapping it with a bandage. Halfway through the process she started to cry. The tears didn't stop and after a while she left me and shut herself up in the bedroom.

When I went to check on her a while later she was fast asleep, her face muddled like an artist's palette from tears.

That night, I had only walked a short distance of the way back from Mitsuko's place when I bumped into Ramen. I wasn't particularly surprised, since he was always hanging around with the hope of snaring Mitsuko. And since he delivered food for a living, he'd be used to finding out where people lived.

"Huh, that's odd. Ghost Girl not with you?" Mitsuko usually accompanied me back to the station. "You're all alone? I'll take you home if you like, missy. Where d'ya live?"

Ramen was dressed in a blue turtleneck sweater, in place of the white broth-stained overalls he always wore for work. The heady rush of excitement I'd felt when I cut Mitsuko's wrist was still there, whizzing inside me with no outlet in sight.

"Really? You'd take me home?"

He looked surprised—it was the first time I'd spoken a word to him.

"Sure, no problem." He was clearly struggling to feign a sullen face in order to hide his delight. I turned around and started to walk away from the station. "Huh? Taking the long way around? So, honey, what's your name? Ah, you can call me Joe."

"I'm Mitsuko."

"So did you guess, Mitsuko? It was you I liked all along, not Ghost Girl. Cross my heart."

Mitsuko's apartment was halfway up a small hill. Going downhill led to the main street and the station, but the way up was an endless stretch of sleepy residential areas. I meandered from corner to corner, making my way upward. Ramen was following behind and whistling in an act of forced nonchalance, but he was starting to get impatient.

"Hey Mitsuko, how far are we going here? It's getting late, so let's hurry back to your place," he said.

We had at some point reached the top and were already walking downhill when Ramen opened his mouth to protest again. That was when I finally caught sight of what I'd been looking for.

Stairs.

I walked to them and stopped, pressing my hands to my knees.

"Mitsuko, are you okay?" Ramen walked over and looked into my face. He still smelled of ramen, even in his blue sweater.

"Just a cramp, in my leg. Can you give me a piggyback ride to the bottom?"

"Carry you? Seriously?"

"Right. I guess you need muscles to…"

"I've got muscles. Okay, sure, I'll carry you. Come on then."

The moment Ramen turned and crouched, I kicked him in the lower back, sending him flying.

His mouth slammed into the steps before he could scream, so the only sound was a choked-off groan. Ramen's body flipped over as it pitched down the steps, finally coming to rest on a landing.

For some reason I didn't feel any of the usual elation, no Nan-Core. My heart was racing madly, but it was nothing more than a routine and purely physical response to what had just happened.

After checking that no one else was around, I walked down the steps and stopped next to him. It was hard to tell if he was still breathing. I lugged his heavy body to the edge of the landing, trying not to look at his acne-covered face, then gathered my strength and kicked him again, sending him down the last half of the steps.

I didn't bother to check on him after that. I climbed back up to the street, feeling cheated somehow as I set off in the general direction of the train station.

Sometime later, I told Mitsuko what had happened when she commented on not having seen Ramen for a while.

"What? Oh, the poor bastard. Did he really die?"

"I didn't check, but…"

"I wonder if it was in the papers."

"Dunno."

"No one will find out?"

"It'll be fine."

A couple of days after that I got Mitsuko to cut my wrist again, twice this time, still hoping she would stop doing it to herself if she got a taste of what it was like to cut other people. But she much preferred it when I cut her, not the other way around. Whenever she cut me she always begged me to do the same for her.

"It's wonderful." After cutting each other she would stretch out her arm, trickling with blood, and shut her eyes in delight.

"If it feels so good I promise I'll do it on your birthday, once a year. But please stop cutting yourself."

"I couldn't wait for a whole year."

"You can't know that unless you try."

"Let's get away from this place, go somewhere together. We could live normal lives, I know it, we just need to be someplace new, somewhere far away."

"Going far away won't change anything."

"We could go north, where everything's white with snow in the winter. We could go all the way to Hokkaido. It'd be like living in a foreign country."

"Okay, Mitsuko, if you're serious, could you promise not to cut yourself for at least two months? Starting today."

"Yeah, I can do that. Two months is fine, absolutely."

Needless to say, I had no intention of following Mitsuko to Hokkaido. Even so, I bought a tourist map of the island and joined her in gazing at the photos of a place that transformed anew with each turn of the seasons. If Mitsuko somehow lasted the two months, my plan was to think up an excuse to add another, then another. I thought there was hope. Her diet was improving gradually, and she was now able to eat most things except meat or fish.

We would rent an apartment in Hakodate and work as waitresses, or as assistants at a florist. I would cook and Mitsuko would do the cleaning. When we had enough money saved we would open a small business that was part cafe, part flower shop. The customers in our cafe would drink coffee and eat cakes, the air smelling of flowers as they looked around and debated which blooms to buy.

We discussed such things tirelessly as the days passed uneventfully and the season transitioned from winter to spring. Mitsuko laughed a lot, and I think she even put on a little weight. She was eagerness personified when she invited me to come with her to Hakodate and scout things out, saying she would pay for the trip. I always found travel to be tedious, but with things as they were it felt like I had no choice but to go. I supposed July would be best if we were to go, so I decided to try every trick in the book to stretch out the two-month period she had originally agreed to.

Early in the final week of those initial two months, Mitsuko was walking by my side when suddenly she collapsed in the middle of the street and lost consciousness.

She hadn't seemed any different from usual, but on closer inspection I saw blood dripping from the cuff of her blouse. A crowd had gathered so there was nothing I could do, and before I knew it we were both in an ambulance that someone had called. The doctor told me she had cut herself at the wrist and inside her elbow, that the cuts had been quite deep, and that it looked like Mitsuko had attempted to stitch the one at her elbow with a needle and thread.

After some time a woman turned up claiming to be Mitsuko's mother. She was dressed in a flawlessly draped pearl-white kimono and gave me a scathing glare as she looked me up and down. I walked out of the hospital.

When I visited Mitsuko's apartment a few days later I found her back in her own bed, already having been discharged.

"I'm sorry, I just couldn't do it."

I was stunned into silence at the fact that she didn't have a trace of makeup on. I could never have imagined how she looked without it. All her features were there, but she looked fragile, like an infant born prematurely. Or like Nana, the aging doll I'd dispatched into the river. Her skin was clammy and bloated, probably from crying herself to sleep over and over again. And it wasn't just her face. Her ears, the body beneath the sheets—it was as though her entire frame had shrunk a full size.

"Mitsuko, why couldn't you keep our promise?"

"I'm a mess, you know that."

"Didn't we have plans to go to Hakodate together?"

"I couldn't stop myself, not for that long."

"Okay. Let's start over."

"I can't anymore."

"Why not?"

"Because I love cutting myself."

Mitsuko avoided looking me in the eye the entire time. Her eyes filled with tears again, as one drop and then another soaked into her pillow.

"You love it? Okay, how exactly?" I asked, keeping my voice as gentle as I could.

Her mysterious, unworldly face showed effort as she searched with all her might for the right words. "It's like… If I don't cut, all these things just… I don't, I don't know." Her high-pitched, child-like voice cut off mid-sentence and she fell silent for a long while. "When I cut myself… In that moment when I'm cutting myself, just for that one moment, it's like everything… everything… evvvrything is so…"

She couldn't seem to find the words that followed, no matter how hard she tried. The corners of her mouth were trembling vi-olently. At long last, she closed her eyes in defeat and began to sob weakly.

I knew what it was that she had been unable to describe. I knew, more specifically, that it was something for which there were no words, that it was because of this I had resorted to calling it Nan-Core, strange as the name was.

"Okay. I won't try to stop you anymore. Cutting is very import-ant to you, I see that now."

In all honesty I think I had known it from the beginning. It was just that some part of me didn't like her methods, her resorting to cutting herself. I had wanted to stop her from doing it that way.

"We can't go to Hakodate now," she said. "It was too good to be true anyway."

"We can. We can go when you're better."

"I don't want to move anymore."

I remained silent.

She spoke again. "I don't want to eat anymore. I don't want to leave this bed."

"Do you want to cut now?" She gave a very slight nod. "Do you want me to do it, like before?" Another nod, almost imperceptible. I asked where she kept the supplies then went to fetch them, leaving her side for a moment. "Hey, Mitsuko. We should still go somewhere together, you know. We could go even farther than Hakodate, farther than Hokkaido. Let's go to another country. Some town we've never even heard of, one day, just the two of us."

As I spoke I placed the plastic bag over her left arm. I used the bag because I wanted to do it her way.

I was certain she understood what was about to happen.

"And in some faraway town, our own little cafe—"

"That's right," I chimed in. "A nice little cafe where you can drink coffee surrounded by the smell of flowers."

I wanted it to be over in one go, so I took the blade and made a long, deep incision, as though I was cleaving her arm in two.

"All the cups, plates, and sugar bowls will be white," she said.

"Yes. That will make the surrounding flowers stand out."

"There's a cowbell ringing at the door, and the happy voices of customers chatting."

"I'm baking cakes and Mitsuko, you're arranging bouquets, so many bouquets. Just how the customers want them."

"And not just roses or carnations…"

"Baby's breath, buttercups, flowers gathered from fields, flowers we don't even know the names of."

The bag was heavy quickly, the blood spurting out with more force than I'd anticipated.

"Ahh, it's wonderful…"

Neither of us spoke further. A bystander would only have seen us looking at each other in silence, but we were in fact caught up together inside a blissful clarity. The nape of my neck where I'd had the lump as a child hardened, throbbing like a powerful drum.

Mitsuko and I were failed people. We were like ugly catfish, living on the bottom of a stagnant swamp. But in moments like this even catfish, ignorant of why they are born that way, manage to float to the water's surface to breathe in clean air and, in the light of the sun, witness the world as it is meant to be seen. Only during such moments were we able to be as normal people.

The afterimage of the world I saw with Mitsuko that day has been burned into my mind. I have no doubt that it will stay with me until the day I die.

Blood spilled from the bag, soaking into the carpet. At some point Mitsuko closed her eyes and drowsed off, but I remained transfixed until the moment that she was truly gone.

That was where the second notebook ended, even though there were plenty of blank pages towards the back. Even if it hadn't stopped there I doubted I could have continued reading.

Still leaning against the window I gasped for air like a

man nearly drowned. A thin film of oily sweat clung to the roots of my hair, face, and back. I couldn't tell myself it was fiction, not anymore. Each line of text conveyed a vividness of the sort that only truth could impart.

Mom, then. Could Mom really have written this?

I had tussled with that question in some corner of my mind the whole time I was reading. Aside from Dad, there was no one else to consider. And hadn't Yohei said it himself? That writing something like that was definitely possible for her?

I covered my face with my hands and pressed my temples hard. I'd run out of energy and couldn't think properly. But I still felt the need to get the facts straight and make sense of it all.

The view outside the window was the same as always. It was a bright, early-summer Sunday. The hydrangeas were in full bloom in the neighbor's garden.

What did it mean if Mom was a murderer?

Had she killed and replaced my real mother?

Was that bundle of hair from my murdered mother?

If so, why was the name Misako, Mom's name, on the paper it was wrapped in?

Had Mom been holding the pillow at my bedside because she'd meant to kill me, too?

What about the fear on her face that time she was shuffling along in Dad's sandals like a sleepwalker?

Had her death really been an accident? Could it possibly have been suicide, repentance for her crimes?

Or had Dad killed her, having discovered what she had done?

Had he known from the beginning?

Of course he had, there was no way he couldn't have. Whatever clandestine dealings had taken place, Mom could never have replaced my real mother and act like it had never happened without first conspiring with Dad.

For the first time ever, I felt pure and absolute terror. Was this reality? Despite having lived with them for such a long time I suddenly felt like I couldn't remember either of their faces. I concentrated my thoughts but only saw a couple of masks, featureless, expressionless, pure white. Who were these people I had always called "Mom" and "Dad"? I shrank in the face of such doubts.

I knew time was short. I checked my watch and saw it was already after five. Assuming he didn't stop anywhere after helping Gran with her dinner, Dad would be home by seven at the latest. Yohei was scheduled to give me a warning call from the station at Yamato Koriyama, so I would be okay until then.

I had finished two of the four notebooks, so I was halfway through. I picked up the notebook marked number three and flicked nervously through the pages. From the first lines, it was evident that some time had passed since the events of the second book. Perhaps because of this, I thought I could make out subtle differences in the penmanship. The writing clearly belonged to the same person but the characters had firmed up somewhat, making them easier to follow.

Maybe it was just the filter of my new preconceptions, but the handwriting didn't look dissimilar to Mom's.

7

I haven't done this for a long time, but I must write again. I had only started out of a need to put Mitsuko's story into words and had considered the task complete. But now I have to tell *you* about everything that came afterwards. It's too painful to keep up the lies. I'm sorry, but I'm going to have to go through everything, slowly, from square one. It's difficult for me to pick out just the relevant points and summarize.

A few years after Mitsuko died, I took an office job at a construction company. I continued with my attempts to blend in, wearing a mask and hoping no one would see it for what it was, but I found office life more lonesome and odd than school. Gone was the freedom I'd had as a student to do nothing, the freedom to pull away from my surroundings when I needed to. I was trading myself for money so I knew there was nothing I could do about having to perform my work, but the way things were structured meant I was forced to interact with people I didn't understand and do things unrelated to the job just to get anything done.

One time we gathered to offer our condolences to a young colleague who had just lost his baby son to cancer. Some said they were too upset to sleep, some said they'd lost their desire to work from dwelling on thoughts about the impermanence of life, others gripped his shoulders and said we were all by his side to help him hang in there. They all wore dark expressions with their brows drawn, and a few of the women had tears in their eyes.

I hid my face behind a handkerchief held over my eyes. This was only because I knew my mask was about to start cracking apart.

I didn't feel like it was strange for them to be so grief-stricken over a child they had never met or for this colleague they weren't particularly close to. What I found odd was the fact that both the consolers and the consoled were all perfectly aware that the whole thing was merely a form of acting. I couldn't see why they would take part in such an unpleasant charade. It wasn't long after the group disbanded that the women gathered in the bathroom, already giggling as they reapplied their mascara.

I made a name for myself as a crybaby. This was because I was so quick to cover my face behind my handkerchief. I used it when one of the female employees was leaving to get married, when everyone was saying things like, "Congratulations! I'm so happy it's like I'm the one who's getting married!" or, "We'll still be best friends after you're married. That'll never change!" I used it whenever there was a work-related conflict and I didn't know whose side to take. I used it when I was simply tired and didn't want anyone to talk to me.

About a year into the job I was forced out.

I loved to spend each day just idling around. I especially enjoyed sitting in the windows of fast-food restaurants or on park benches, getting lost in watching people come and go. I would be aware of everything around me, but it felt like the core part of my mind had fallen asleep. It was like a waking dream, and I would see all sorts of things.

The Nan-Core that was Mitsuko stayed with me, the vividness not fading in the slightest. Her ruby blood flowed eternally from the cut on her wrist, her eyes gazing eternally into mine. The others were all there inside her: Nana, Michiru, the dead boy with his neck trapped in the park grate.

Ramen wasn't there at first. I think that was probably because I hadn't felt any kind of attachment to him. Because I'd hated him. Then, one day, I was sitting near the flow of people, the core of my mind having just fallen into its usual trance when, even though I'd forgotten all about him, he popped into my head. I can't say why. My dreams were free creatures. They did what they wanted, living according to their own free will.

Ramen was in his white overalls as he came over on his moped, the apparatus to carry deliveries hanging over the luggage rack.

"Hey there, lady," he said, riding up next to me as he put a foot on the ground. "So, what's the deal? Why am I the only one you don't let in? That's so mean, leaving me out like that."

It came back to me then, how he'd smelled of ramen broth when he turned to give me a piggyback. And, just like that, he became a part of Mitsuko, too.

I sometimes wished I'd been arrested for murder. Not because I felt guilt. I never felt anything like that at all. But I don't think I could tell you why, even if you asked me.

I still don't know why Mitsuko and Ramen's deaths were settled so easily. I wondered what the police were doing. Had they done the proper checks for fingerprints or searched for other evidence? Had they even realized they were dealing with murder cases in the first place?

I had tampered with things in Mitsuko's case, that was true. I, too, have instincts for self-preservation. More so than the death penalty, it was the thought of being locked up in a tiny, cage-like room that really scared me. It was so terrifying I feared just thinking about it would drive me crazy.

That was why I took the used blade and plastic bag home with me, and why I chose a different blade from her collection and left it in the puddle of blood. Even then I knew my attempt at a cover-up was nothing more than a gesture to ease my mind. My prints were all over the rest of her apartment, and a good number of people knew Mitsuko and I were close. If the police had been serious, their investigations would have turned up any number of anomalies.

I read something recently that said only a tiny percent of un-natural deaths get court-ordered autopsies. That made me wonder if the police were actually trying to avoid admitting that a murder was a murder. Perhaps homicide rates in most cities are actually much higher, but as with Mitsuko and Ramen, many of the cases are taken care of without ever surfacing.

Every day I walked aimlessly through the crowds and even then I felt distant and separate from everyone else. In the city you can get by for a whole week or two without having to say a single word to anyone. When I wasn't using my voice I would get wrapped up in this sensation of peace and feel like my vocal cords were qui-etly atrophying.

I don't remember exactly when it was, but one day I sat down on a park bench in the middle of the day and found myself still sitting there after it was dark out. It was well into the night when I at last got to my feet and started to amble towards the road. That was when an older-looking man leaning against a car called out from beyond the exit.

"I've seen you hanging around here a lot recently. How much?" he asked. When I didn't respond he said, "Right, whatever, hop in," climbing into the car before me. He was acting and talking very naturally and didn't seem anything like my old work colleagues.

I knew the man had misread the situation, but I didn't mind since he said he would pay me for it. It had been a while since I'd quit my old job, and I was having a hard time getting by.

He took me to a room, and no matter what he did to me I simply figured that was the way these things worked, and stayed quiet the whole time. He said it was the first time he'd slept with a virgin prostitute and gave me lots of money. I decided then that I was a fit for that sort of job, more so than some sort of office work. Both types of jobs involved me trading myself for money—the only difference was which part I put on sale. I found the sensation of flesh bumping into flesh unpleasant, but it beat the agony of having to hide behind a handkerchief because I couldn't pretend to be a normal person.

I soon found myself getting used to what to do. When I needed money, I just walked up to men in the street at night and said, "What time is it?" Many just ignored me, and some refused to pay even after they'd become clients. Still, the great thing about the work was how it didn't set limits on my time. I only worked when I wanted and was otherwise free to laze around like before.

The sex… Well, it felt almost like I was being taken apart. Basically, it felt like the flesh I put on sale was being disassembled while I was still alive. I got used to it over time, but the sense that the act was bizarre and grotesque never went away. But I never really suffered.

It reminds me now of how I'd done much the same thing with my doll Nana years earlier, opening her up in whichever way I'd wanted.

I also learned that all men are failures. They have such powerful, potentially self-destructive lust all for the tiny moment of pleasure during ejaculation. It's completely out of proportion. Don't they ever realize the contradiction and feel it's totally absurd? Yet it's because men are the way they are that people are able to get by as prostitutes.

I continued to trade my body, switching districts now and then to avoid bumping into the same client more than a few times. My work was out of public view, conducted alone with each client, so it wouldn't have been hard to kill one of them if I'd wanted to, but they were failed people who had nothing but my contempt and I knew killing them wouldn't do anything for me.

Even so, a lot happened during the few years I worked as a prostitute.

One night in winter, I had just asked a passerby for the time, and the pregnant silence that followed made it evident he'd understood my meaning. I took another look and realized he was one of the subsection chiefs from my old job. It was the man that had grabbed his bereaved colleague's shoulder and shaken it, telling him to keep on going.

"Oh, wow, what happened? You've lost so much weight I almost didn't recognize you," he said.

I hadn't been feeling very well since starting sex work, so I surely had lost weight. I was always covered in bruises and small cuts, like a gymnast, even though my clients never actively abused me. Still, none of that shook my conviction that the job was better than anything else out there.

I said, "Well, what'll it be? Are we going someplace, or have you changed your mind?"

"Erm, I... This is what you're really doing now? Yikes." He used the tip of his index finger to scratch at the hairline above his forehead. On his face was a soft, very human expression of the sort he would never have shown at work. "Right, it's cold so we should at least get you out of here. Let's grab a cab."

When we were inside the taxi he pulled out three 10,000-yen notes, and when I took them he reached down and pushed his hand up my skirt. I put the money in my bag and spread my legs.

"Looks like things have been hard for you, too," he said.

I had expected him to take me to some low-rent hotel, but when we got out of the taxi we were outside the multi-use building that housed my old office.

"I can't imagine anyone's still working at this hour."

The office was on the second floor and the windows were all dark, the lights off inside. We walked up the stairwell and our footsteps echoed over the sound of our damp breath.

"I've wanted to try it for a while. On one of the desks in here."

The subsection chief opened the door and I stepped into the deserted office that smelled of dust and plastic. The glow of the streetlights poked through gaps in the blinds, setting off the interior of the office with a pallid glow.

"As cramped as ever, huh? Right, which of the girl's desks to do it on…"

I followed him from behind, picking my way through the rows of desks, when I saw a cylindrical wastepaper bin next to someone's chair. I grabbed it with no particular plan or purpose.

That was when the thought of killing him flashed into my head for the first time.

I swung the bin over my head, ignoring everything spilling out, and swung it down into the head of the man in front of me. I felt resistance, hard then soft, and the man crumpled noiselessly to the floor, his hands trapped behind his back as he had just begun to remove his coat.

I stood there in a daze. I knew I'd done it, but it had happened too quickly. Of course there was no Nan-Core, not from killing like that. Instead I just felt terrible, like I'd betrayed myself and somehow disgraced Mitsuko's death. I'm sure nothing would have happened if it wasn't for that garbage bin; the subsection chief would have taken me to a desk and disassembled me, as always.

Before leaving I drove the base of the bin into his head a couple more times, wanting to make sure he wouldn't start breathing again. I stopped halfway down the stairwell, then, after a moment's deliberation, returned to the office and used the scarf I'd worn over my hair to clean my prints from the bin and the door handle.

There was another time when I killed someone like this, on the spur of the moment. That night I was with a first-time client. For no particular reason I took up a plaster statue of Venus in the room and smashed it into the man's head as he slept. I can't really think of anything I need to write about him, since I don't even remember his face.

What I really hated was that I had gotten into the habit of killing people even when it had nothing to do with a sense of Nan-Core.

I still have the thought each time the media reports the arrest of a serial killer: another one who is possessed by the habit of killing. I wondered if the various issues listed in the papers like parental neglect during youth or physical or mental handicaps had really caused them to make a habit of murder.

They all received death sentences.

It would have been better for us—these people, myself—if we had been born during Japan's Warring States period. It was a time when being a hero meant becoming addicted to murder, to killing as many people as you could; it was your duty to kill the enemy even if they were people you'd never seen before. I'm sure it was the same during the two World Wars and other times like that. Nations with conflicting interests encouraged murder and awarded medals to those who would normally receive the death penalty.

After I hit the man with the figure of Venus I didn't bother wiping off my prints, and I was sure the hotel cameras had images of me even though I had done my best to hide my face, a habit I'd developed because of the type of work I did. But I was never arrested, and I really can't say why. It would have been right for me to have been caught. I didn't feel guilt, but I knew it was wrong for people like me to be left alive. Not in this time and place.

I only had vague feelings on the above issues, though, since I didn't give them any real thought.

There was another night, just like the others, when I called out to a man, also like the others. It was near the entrance to the park where the elderly man had first mistaken me for a prostitute.

"Do you have the time?"

He'd been walking with his eyes trained on the ground but stopped and checked his watch, answering straightaway, "Uhm, it's quarter past nine."

A response like that usually signaled a lack of interest. On any other day I would have backed off silently, but I had just been shooed away by two other men I'd approached.

"Do you have the time?" I repeated, ignoring his first reply.

"Uh, like I said, it's quarter past—" He stopped mid-sentence, his face stiffening with surprise. He had finally worked out what was happening. He clamped his lips shut and tried to walk past me.

"I need money," I said to his retreating back.

It was the truth. I was all but out of money to cover my living costs. To my surprise the man stopped and turned to walk back towards me, a hand rummaging through his pockets. He checked through a tired-looking wallet, then pulled out a single 5,000-yen note.

"I don't have much myself. This is all I can really manage."

He held out the bill and looked at me properly for the first time. A look of surprise crossed his features. I think it was because of how gaunt I had become. I certainly wasn't as far gone as Mitsuko had been, but I was getting thinner by the day despite the fact that I wasn't ill. Because I was so thin I was finding it hard to get clients and had started to really struggle with money.

"So, uhm, are you…okay? You look pretty pale." He stared hesitantly into my face. "Are you maybe…really hungry?"

I didn't say anything.

"Oh, damn. Okay, let's see. Uhm… There's this restaurant I go to all the time, just down the road. It's cheap. Would you like to go?"

I could tell from his demeanor that he hadn't thought it through before speaking and that he immediately regretted his words. But I thanked him anyways and started to follow him. I didn't actually feel hungry, but I went along because I figured I might be able to turn him into a client if I played things right after we'd eaten. I was so desperate for cash I would have let him disassemble me for another 5,000 yen.

The man seemed to be in low spirits, but he introduced himself as he walked and turned back every now and then to check I was still there. He offered small encouragements like, "Not long now," or, "Just around the next corner," and began to walk a touch more briskly.

We approached a short crosswalk and I was about to step into the road when I felt the man's arm press against my chest, like a crossing gate.

"Careful!"

I had been on autopilot when I had walked into his arm and pulled back slightly to see a taxi rush right before my eyes. He checked to the left and the right, still holding me back so I didn't jump out, then finally pulled his crossing-gate-arm away.

It was the first time anyone had done something like that for me.

I crossed the crosswalk.

"There it is. The food's pretty decent considering how cheap it is."

I could see a small diner down the street. A split curtain hung over the entrance and the air smelled of broth. Already by then the awareness was growing inside me that I didn't want this particular man to disassemble me. And perhaps taking the place of something else, I felt a warm rush of saliva along with something I had forgotten for a long time: hunger.

In the numb half-awake, half-asleep daydreams that came to me the next day and the day after, and as I sat in various places around the city absorbed in the flow of people, I saw the arm holding me back like a crossing gate.

Careful, came the whisper.

Careful, careful, careful... I heard his voice over and over, his arm pressing me back over and over.

It had come between me and the car as it shot by, and now, with the same casual ease, it also held me apart from other things, all the nameless, warped objects that were everywhere around me, from the life-sucking void in Michiru's garden, and even from myself when I found I was being drawn inexorably towards the darkness within that void. *Careful*, it said, pulling me back. These things kept happening in my dreams.

I got lost in those dreams, intoxicated, only now and then coming back to myself to gnaw at the chapped skin around my cuticles.

It took about a week to use up the man's 5,000 yen. He was there when I visited the park that night, sitting on one of the short stone pillars at the entrance. He hurried over when he caught sight of me.

"Oh, good, I was afraid you wouldn't come back. Good evening." He stood facing me, keeping a few feet away. "So…" He alternately worried his upper and lower lips, working out what to say. I had never turned down a client before, but I had decided I would say no if he asked to pay for my services. I think he must have seen through my thoughts.

"Oh no, it's nothing like that." He waved his hand in front of his face, flustered. "I was wondering if you'd like to go back to the same place for dinner. The idea came to me earlier. You were eating with such relish, I thought maybe I could take you there every now and then…"

"Thank you," I said just like the first time and followed him there.

After that night he made a habit of taking me out for dinner every few days. Each time I was careful to stop before the pedestrian crossing, making sure to avoid a repeat of what happened the first time. He didn't speak much during our meals, or in general. His expression made it seem like he was concentrating on a sound only he could hear.

Aside from paying for the food he sometimes tried to give me a 5,000-yen note, but I turned him down each time.

"Why? You took some money the first time," he said once, sounding irritated. We were back in the park after dinner and were about to go our separate ways.

"That was because I was planning to work for it."

"So you won't take anything if I don't ask you to work for it?"

"You're always buying me dinner."

"Okay… But what do you normally do for food? Can't say you're putting on any weight."

I fell silent.

"Well, I'm going to ask you to do some work. Five thousand yen's worth. I'm afraid that's the most I can afford right now."

I felt goosebumps prickle up on my back and arms. That surprised me. "I can't."

"Why not?"

"I can't, not with you."

I felt strange as soon as I gave my answer. It only took a moment to understand why. I had never thought of someone as simply "you" before. I think it really was the first time. That was why I came close to being drowned by the unique sensation that came from saying it. My clients were clients, Mitsuko was Mitsuko. I used first names for acquaintances and terms like "Miss" for people I didn't know. Teachers, cab drivers, and police officers I addressed as "sir" or "ma'am." My mother was "Mom." It seemed strange to me; I'd never intentionally avoided using a more familiar form of address. It felt like a switch being flipped on, like there had always been a place inside me set aside for the word, and "you" fit perfectly.

Only this particular man. You alone were you.

"Ah, don't misunderstand me. When I say 'work,' I don't mean *that* kind of work," you added quickly, then explained, "I'm having trouble sleeping again, and it's getting to me. Reading or drinking just makes it worse, and my mind goes to dark places when I'm awake in the middle of the night. So if it's not a hassle, could I ask you to come to my place and sit by my bed, just for an hour or so? I think it might help me sleep to have someone there. I know, it's like I'm a scared little kid. Don't worry, I won't ask for a bedtime story or anything."

I accepted a 5,000-yen note and followed you through the dark streets to your apartment. I lingered a half-step behind to look at the profile of the person who had become you.

Your apartment was nicer than mine but it was still just a shabby single room. You switched on the heater and we had a glass of warm, sweet milk each, then you climbed into bed.

"See? Just like a kid. My parents died in an accident when I was in grade school, and from that shock I can tell some part of my mind remained child-like."

The room was warm and I myself started to feel sleepy as I sat by your bed. You were silent for long periods, speaking only in brief sentences when you did, your voice growing increasingly muffled.

"How old are you?"

I hadn't ever thought about my age. I guessed I was something like twenty-two but I couldn't be sure, so I told you the date I was born instead.

"So…five years younger than me."

"You look…" You had your eyes closed, so I could watch your face as much as I wanted.

"I look…?" you prompted, eyes still closed.

"You look…tired."

"Could you put your hand on my forehead for a little bit?"

I did as you said.

"Ah, that's nice. The human hand is a strange thing. Feels like it's drawing out the pain."

Tiny particles of air tingled, vibrating between my hand and your forehead.

"Mom used to do this when I stayed home from school with a cold. My fever would go right down, didn't need any medicine. Her hand felt like it was magic…" You snored a little, then twitched awake. "Oh, could you turn off the heater when you go? No need to lock the door. And…thank you for this."

After that we continued to have dinner together at the small diner and I would help you sleep when you needed it.

The first thing I did every night was visit the park to check if you were there. On nights when I couldn't find you I would go somewhere else and approach men, asking the time. You knew I was still selling myself on days we didn't meet. Sometimes I couldn't work when you asked me to sit at your bed for a few days in a row, but on such occasions you always made sure to give me a 5,000-yen note. This was you, but I needed the income.

You said there were periods that came every couple of months when your insomnia became unbearable. It was at the beginning of these periods that you seemed to suffer the most. You turned pale like you were ill, bags forming under your eyes, and stayed silent longer than usual. Sometimes you would still be awake after I'd been with you for two or three hours, and when that happened you apologized and told me I could leave. Most of the time, however, you told me about little things from your childhood as your voice grew nearly inaudible, and you managed to sleep for a little while, even if you woke again before morning.

As I watched you, asleep and defenseless, I entertained myself with thoughts about how I would kill you. It was the only conclusion I understood in a relationship like ours. The act of killing was the only way I knew of getting closer to another person.

It was only the money that stopped me from doing it there and then. I made an effort not to kill men who gave me money. I told myself I didn't have any reason to kill you, not while you kept giving me those 5,000-yen notes. I know my reasoning was foolish. But whenever I tried to think deeply about the phenomenon that you were, I experienced a sudden, uncontrollable rush of anxiety and confusion. I would end up completely muddled.

Your eyes shut reflexively when I put my hand on your forehead, but one night they came open again and you looked up at me from your bed.

"I've been wondering why I feel so relaxed around you." Your eyes were a mysterious color that night. I'd read in a book once about a color called hazel. I think that's what they were. "It's some kind of atonement, right? You're trying to make up for doing something bad, that's why you're a prostitute?"

That was the first time you'd ever said "prostitute." I pulled my hand back from your forehead.

"That's what it is," you said. "We're both sinners. That's why we're in tune with each other."

"I don't think so. I've never atoned for anything."

"So I'm wrong…" You looked away to glare at the ceiling as though something was hiding in there. "But you've noticed that I'm really odd, right? Don't you think it's weird that I haven't tried to sleep with you, even after all these nights together?"

"Because I said I couldn't when I first met you."

"I'd try regardless, if I wanted to."

"Then it's because I'm a dirty whore."

"No! It's nothing like that. Could I… Could I tell you about the sin I committed? I haven't ever told anyone about it."

"Please. Tell me whatever you want."

"I killed someone. A child."

"I've killed as well. Four, maybe five people."

"Ha ha. Are you just trying to make me feel better by saying that?"

"No. It's the truth."

You ignored me and furrowed your eyebrows tight, trying to work up the strength to say what you needed to.

"I'm…impotent," you spat, then clamped your lips shut again. Then you continued, the words rushing out. "I can't sleep and I can't have sex, all because of what I did."

I couldn't tell if you were suffering because of the impotence or because of the sin thing in your past, but I realized that I was impotent in some way as well and decided that was why it felt like we were on the same wavelength.

But what you said next caught me completely off guard. The kid you'd killed had been a small boy of eleven years. You told me how, years ago, you'd tried to help a boy who had been trying to recover a hat that had fallen into a roadside gutter; how you'd lifted up the heavy iron grate but after a while couldn't handle the weight any longer; and how you dropped it on the kid whose head was still inside the mouth of the gutter.

Could such a thing even be possible?

"Where did this happen?"

I already knew your answer before you told me. I was covered in a sheen of sweat, making my skin feel slimy and frog-like. All my emotions back then had been intensely drawn towards the boy on the brink of death. For the man holding up the grate, instead of his face I mostly remembered his trembling and bunched-up muscles along his neck and arms. I recalled that he'd had long, wavy hair that fell to his shoulders.

"What happened afterwards?"

"They ruled it involuntary manslaughter, and I was given a suspended sentence. I managed to pay the settlement by selling the property my parents left me. I was left without a yen to my name but was allowed to live freely, as you see me now."

Was there a connection between that incident and the fact that you had become you? It was surely your guilty conscience that had caused you to give five thousand yen to me, a mere passerby, that first night. So does that mean we would never have known each other if you hadn't committed that sin?

"When I close my eyes to try and sleep I see his thin legs on the backs of my eyelids. I see those legs when I'm on top of a woman, no matter how hard I try to lose myself in the act. I can see his blue sneakers as his legs spasm, kicking one last time into the ground."

I knew what guilt was in theory, but I'd never witnessed first-hand anyone suffering from it.

"The kid's little sister saw it all. I was told she started to have bad panic attacks after that. It wasn't just her. Their mother and father, too... The wounds I gave them won't heal for the rest of their lives. There was another girl there, too. Probably middle-school age, although I was too caught up to properly see her face. She was passing by and tried to lend a hand, holding up the grate. Even then I couldn't..."

"What happened to her?"

"She was gone by the time I thought to look. She must have been terrified. She was just a passerby, yet I did something regrettable to her. She, too, was probably so damaged she never recovered."

There was an odd feeling of something itchy and unpleasantly warm spreading in my lungs, making me feel like I couldn't breathe properly. When I sucked in some air as deeply as I could my throat trembled like I was panting. By the way you looked I realized that guilt, the sense of having done something wrong, could be so intense as to tear a person to shreds.

"The other girl is fine."

"How could you know that?"

"Well, what I mean is, if she was someone weak-willed, she wouldn't have tried to help with something so dangerous. So I'd say she's pretty strong."

You stared at me for a while, looking mystified. Then you unfolded your arms and reached out, gently placing a palm on my cheek.

"Thanks. You really are very sweet."

It was around then that I started to feel ill. Nothing I did seemed to help. I became completely hypersensitive and didn't want to do anything. It was like being constantly motion sick.

I couldn't eat anything at our usual place—just the smell of food I caught from ducking under the entryway curtain was enough to make me retch.

You were the one to suggest that I might be pregnant. It wasn't unusual for me to miss periods so I hadn't given it much thought. Besides, I always used contraceptives at work. That was only because my clients were scared of catching something. The idea of getting pregnant had always seemed completely irrelevant to me, whether I used a condom or not. I was a vessel, but I was already full—with Mitsuko and Michiru, with the boy you thought you'd killed, with Ramen and the others.

Yet it happened anyway. I was pregnant despite not knowing

who the father was or how I'd slipped up. How disappointingly easy it is to get pregnant.

I refrained from seeing a doctor even after I was sure of my condition. I figured that any seed that had taken root in my worn-out body would get flushed away soon enough. More importantly, I didn't have the money for an abortion.

I was amazed to find out that you were considering something completely different.

"Let's marry. We can get married and raise the kid together," you said.

We were in your room one night and we were sitting opposite each other, drinking milk before you went to bed. I felt my throat clench painfully.

"I can't. I can't have a child."

"Why not?"

"I can't be someone's mother. That's too strange. I'm afraid bad stuff might happen later on if I act weird."

"Weird or no, you'll still be a mother when the baby's born."

"It won't be born. I'm sure I'll miscarry."

"No, don't say that. We've been gifted with this baby. It's fate, it has to be. Let's raise it together."

You said "fate" with a kind of solemnity, like the word itself was special. You'd decided it was providence: You had taken the life of one child, so you would raise another whose paternity was unknown. Does fate amount to forgiveness of one's sins? Is fate the same as my Nan-Core? But does something like destiny really exist? Were you my destiny? I was seized by a type of chaos I'd never experienced before you entered my life.

Little by little, my stomach swelled. I was no longer able to keep working. On the day we officially registered our marriage, you gave me a ring with a little blue stone. A keepsake from your mother, you said. By then we were already living together, sharing a small three-room apartment, and you had managed to leverage your qualifications to land a job with a proper company. Just like that, you put an end to your life of dropping in and out of part-time work.

The baby was born on a rainy morning.

My phone rang. The display said it was a payphone but I knew it was Yohei.

"What is it, where are you calling from?" Jolted by the sudden return to reality, my tone came out sharp and demanding.

"The hell is your problem, man. You sound like you're being strangled."

"Why are you calling me from a payphone?"

"Because I'm still at Gran's. They don't allow mobiles here. Lots of people with pacemakers and things."

"And Dad?"

"He said he wasn't feeling too good so he just left. He said there'd be taxis out front so he'd catch one of those and go home. I hope he's all right. He was kind of pale, I think he was feeling sick."

I remembered how ill he'd looked just a few hours earlier when I'd seen him from the window of the coffee shop, but I didn't have time to start worrying about that. "Exactly how long ago did he leave?" I asked, shaking the notebook impatiently.

"About ten minutes?"

"You… Why didn't you call me right away?"

"I couldn't help it. Dad passed the baton to me so I had to look after Gran. I couldn't leave her alone and make a call in the middle of dinner, could I? It's hard enough to make her eat as it is."

"Fine. I'm hanging up now."

"So, think you'll get through the notebooks? It already sounds like you've found some more crazy bullshit," he snickered. "Anyways, you can flip out all you like, just don't forget your promise. Eight o'clock, same steakhouse as last time."

It was already a little after six. Dad was coming from the nursing home, and assuming he had gotten into a cab ten minutes ago it would be another twenty or so before he was back. I decided to play it safe and leave in ten. I resolved to read until time was up and let my eyes trace over the characters on the page, but I was nervous and jumpy and couldn't absorb their meaning.

It felt like I'd been forced into a dead end. If I wanted to keep reading, was there nothing to do but repeat this process the next Sunday? I knew I couldn't wait that long. I was on the third notebook, almost at the end. After a moment's hesitation I decided to take just the third one with me.

I couldn't know if Dad was planning to check on the notebooks during the coming week, but even if he was, I had a hunch he wouldn't actually bother taking them out of the manila envelope. At least, I prayed that he wouldn't.

Before sliding the other notebooks into the envelope I picked up the notebook marked four and flipped through the pages. The first third had writing, but the rest were blank. Temptation got the better of me and I scanned the last few lines. The writing was chaotic and each sentence was followed by a large gap.

You won't let me live.

You killing me is my only salvation.

Because you are my you—

Please, don't ever forget that.

But if some enchantment, like that which I felt when you spoke of fate, were to bring me back and you were to take me in your arms again, I would like to have another child. It would be your true child, one that will take the place of this child that I am going to kill.
That is my wish.

The writing ended there. I didn't have time to dwell on it so I gathered three of the notebooks and slipped them into the envelope before putting it back in the box, then closed the closet door. After checking I hadn't left anything that would give my presence away I left the study. I made a beeline for the front door, as single-minded as I had been on the way in, and got into my shoes.

8

I took the long route through side streets on my way back to the station, not wanting to bump into Dad's taxi. I went into the coffee shop I'd used to watch out for Dad earlier, and just as I leaned into one of the chairs, some thread of tension within me finally snapped, causing my mind to momentarily go blank.

I asked for coffee when a girl came to take my order and remembered—feeling oddly as though it was someone else's business—that it was time for Shaggy Head to start closing down for the day. I knew I should call in, but it felt like too much of a hassle, so I ended up just gazing aimlessly around the shop's busy interior.

In my mind, I retraced the final lines I'd skimmed over in the study.

You killing me... This child that I am going to kill.

The phrasing seemed simple, but somehow too vague. It wasn't clear what sequence of events had led the author to believe she was going to be killed, nor whether the child she was going to kill was the baby she had given birth to on the rainy morning. I was almost finished with the third notebook, but I still couldn't make out the overall picture. There was only one thing I thought I knew for sure: that the man the narrator

113

called "you" was my Dad.

As evidence, there was the account of the man losing his parents in an accident while still in elementary school. That was a perfect fit for Dad. He had been in second grade when he lost his parents in a major plane crash, and after that he was raised by a spinster aunt on his mother's side. Also, the fact that the man had used his "qualifications" to find work was another match. Dad held a number of certificates in book-keeping.

I think I would have still realized the man was Dad even without such details to help put things together. It was completely natural for the two men to overlap and become one: this man who had raised a kid as his own without knowing who the father was, and my father, who stared with dark eyes at photographs of abused children as though he was the one responsible for their suffering.

The problem was the author. It was either Mom or my real mother. I couldn't tell which, but I was certain it was one or the other. There was definitely a part where the narrator was said to be five years younger than the man. I knew for a fact that Mom was five years younger than Dad. But it wasn't proof if the two women—Mom, and my real mother—happened to be the same age. Had the narrator really died, as intimated in the closing section? Or had she continued to live, later to give birth to "your" (Dad's) child?

Thinking about it was only wasting time.

I was about to open the notebook when I saw that the coffee I'd ordered was sitting near the edge of the table. It was already getting cold. I took a sip and began to read the remainder of the text.

The baby was born on a rainy morning.

Born at last to an impotent father and a prostitute mother. It was a boy, and I'm sure that only served to strengthen your belief in fate. I was still in a daze, overwhelmed by the abnormality of what had happened to my body, and looked on as you gingerly took the baby into your arms.

The birthing process had been a disassembly that justified the term far more than any of the other experiences I'd had in the past. I thought my body had split in half to let the baby out. It was over, though, and I had somehow returned to my usual shape.

"He's so small," you said then fell quiet, never taking your eyes off the baby. There was a smile playing at the corners of your mouth.

Through the window I could see it was raining hard, but I couldn't hear anything. As I started to fall asleep I felt strangely comforted, feeling like your smile was actually for me and not the baby.

After the baby was born the ghosts that haunted me seemed to fall away. I felt empty for a while, as though everything that had been inside me until that point, even Mitsuko and Michiru, had exited me. I was amazed at how easy it was to breathe when I found myself so empty.

Being a prostitute hadn't been too bad, but it was easier to be a mother. It suited me. I didn't have anything specific to do except wait for you to come home, so I spent whole days just watching the baby. I had never observed anything with such enthusiasm. It was something that had come from inside of me, so I wanted to discern whether it was a part of me or an extension of myself.

If I noted any changes I informed you when you returned in the evening from work. When the baby had puckered his lips during a bath, or kicked at his sheets, or when the tip of a small tooth had become visible, for example.

I liked the look on your face when you listened to these reports. Come dinner you took a sip of beer and said things like, "The leaves are all gone from the row of gingko trees, it really is winter already."

I liked the way you looked those times. I liked the way you looked when you opened your eyes in bed at night to whisper, "Listen, it's started to rain," despite the loneliness that seeped through your expression. Whenever words like "gingko" or "winter" or "rain" crossed your lips, I felt like I was getting closer to understanding their true forms which I didn't know.

We slept in one bed and made as little physical contact as possible, but sometimes we woke to find our hands or legs entangled of their own accord. The baby's cot was in the same room, and he wriggled and cried and moaned throughout the night, but before we knew it, your insomnia had gone away.

I can't say if the same could be said of your guilt.

Of course, you never should have had to bear that guilt in the first place. I was the one who took the boy's life. I was the one who tricked you, who led you to wrongfully conclude it was your fault. Because of the guilt I had planted inside of you, you gave me money, took me to your little diner, even married me so we could stay together. Our life was built on mistaken guilt, and so long as that remained the case, everything about it was wrong.

I knew that something needed to be done, but each time I tried to think it through I only got confused.

I couldn't figure it out, so I stopped thinking about it.

Our baby began to make noises like "Waah" and "Mmama"

and learned how to crawl around the room. You brought a nev-er-ending stream of toys home. One night you gave him a small tambourine with a picture on it. He absolutely loved it and started to bang it into whatever was around, filling the room with the lively noise.

When he finally tried whacking it on his own face, you laughed out loud. "I never get tired of watching this little guy," you said.

Having banged the tambourine into his face a few times it apparently started to hurt, and when he opened his mouth to cry you quickly scooped him up and shook the instrument in a steady rhythm.

"Right, how about we sing along with Daddy. Okay? Waaa, waaa, waaah…"

It was the middle of dinner but you cuddled him close as you paced around the room. You rocked his little frame up and down, occasionally kissing him on the forehead, and each time you did so I felt my own forehead tingle.

By the time you got back to the table with the baby, mood restored, on your knee, you were short of breath. You scraped a spoonful of fish from your plate and tried to put it in his mouth, but he was full and turned his face away in a sulk. When you tried to eat it instead his elbow bumped into you, like he'd done it on purpose, sending the contents of the spoon all over your nose.

"Oof! Argh, you little critter."

The baby cackled with laughter. You blinked a few times, as some of the food had gotten into your eyes, then burst into laughter right along with him. I hurriedly held out a box of tissues.

"Y-You got me good, little scallywag." You wiped a little dribble from the baby's mouth. "Ah, this is so much fun," you mumbled.

Then your hand stopped moving and you stared at me with

those mysterious hazel eyes. I think I'd been sitting with my mouth hanging open like a fool. I'd just had the sudden realization that the pleasant sensation I'd been feeling, like my heart was expanding outwards in all directions, was what it felt like to have fun. I felt like I was inflating, ready to bounce into the air like a hot-air balloon, and the sensation was tinged with a hint of anxiety that I might expand too far and burst open. I had of course heard the word "fun" before, but I had never once experienced it for myself. It felt like everything in the room was covered in a glowing aura, making everything appear brand-new.

"Fun" felt a little bit like Nan-Core.

I'll never forget the beggarweed, either. That happened when we went out on a walk—a little farther than usual to visit a shrine—with you pushing the baby buggy along. We had just completed a lap of the narrow paths that circled the grounds and were about to head back home. Then we noticed all the dry, brown, triangular pods stuck to our sweaters.

"Beggarweed seeds. Damn, these things are a pain," you said, starting to pull at the seeds covering your arm. I was pulling some from my skirt when I glanced at the baby, asleep inside the buggy, and saw that some had gotten into his hair. I pulled some out then went back to work on myself, but it was never-ending.

"Quite a job, isn't it?" Your hand popped up and picked some seeds off the back of my shoulder. When you finished there you moved on to my back, my hair, to my side. You said, "Here they are, and here," never noticing the way my body was tensing up.

Your cuff brushed into me and I picked a seed from there, too. It was stuck in the little fibers of your flannel shirt, and it refused to come out easily. I carried on trying, feeling a rush of determination, and picked off even more of the seeds, another, and another. There was an infinite number of seeds.

We stood there for a long time, engrossed in the task of picking seeds off each other, and as we did, we began to gradually dissolve and become one, my hand becoming your hand, your body becoming my body. After we'd picked off the last seeds and started to walk again, you joked that the beggarweed would be bursting with blossoms next fall right there along the path and that we'd probably get covered with seeds all over again.

One night about a year later, you embraced me in bed. I felt like I'd turned into a baby, probably because of the many times I'd held ours, keeping still just as you were then.

Enclosed in the warmth of your body I closed my eyes, feeling completely protected in your arms—my crossing gates. The truth is I wanted us to stay like that forever, but after a while you began to undo the buttons along my collar, whispering, "It's gonna be all right." I wasn't sure if you were talking about your impotency. I had told myself that there wasn't a single reason for you to feel attracted to my body, so your impotency would never be cured.

You were trembling. Or maybe I was the one who was trembling.

I was afraid. I knew that what was about to happen would be totally different from the disassembly that I knew so well, yet I was afraid all the same. Or maybe that was exactly why I was afraid.

There was a strange magnetism passing between my skin and your hands before you even touched me. It was like they were calling out to each other. Your hand touched my chest first. When you touched me, all the parts of my body you weren't touching began to call out, too. I became full of calling voices, my fear quickly ebbing away.

When I took off my clothes my body was teeming with tiny beggarweed seeds. The countless seeds itched against my skin all over, waiting to be picked off by your fingers. No matter how many you picked off, a ceaseless stream of new seeds appeared in their place. If you hadn't touched me that wouldn't have happened. You needed to pick me apart and pick me apart until none of me remained.

Gradually I weakened, reaching a point where I could no longer prevent my body from opening up. Before I knew it I had transformed into Mitsuko, and I held my arm out to you. I held out every possible thing to you. *Come on. Cut me. Please... Come on.*

My wish was granted. You were mercilessly kind. You made a deep incision and my body gushed out from within itself. I was dying, endlessly. As you killed me, a pure rush of life-force burst into flames. The higher the flames rose, the more we became fused together.

Oh, it was so pleasurable. How wonderful it would have been for Mitsuko to have experienced it, too.

I begged to be kept frozen in that moment forever, but time restarted all the same. I opened my eyes. It felt strange to come back to it all within your arms. Even though Mitsuko was still dead.

"Don't cry," you said.

I hadn't been crying, but when I touched my face I was stunned to find it wet.

"When he's a little bigger, let's give him a brother or a sister. I think he'd like that."

We didn't talk about what had just happened. I didn't know how to express the fact that you'd become even more you than before. Here and there my body still tingled. A long breath escaped from between your teeth and after a little while you were asleep, still holding me in your arms.

You insisted that we should visit my parents. You'd said as much when we registered our marriage, but I hadn't been able to bring myself to want to go.

"I don't know what happened between you and them, but they'll understand if we explain everything properly."

"Nothing happened, not really."

"Then why not? I'd imagined you'd had some terrible experience with your family or something like that." It was the first time you'd asked about my past.

"I just don't want to see them."

"Okay, but why not?"

It was only when you asked me that I realized I didn't know the answer myself. I'd left home when I had started my corporate job, then moved a couple of times since then and hadn't given them my latest address. That was all it was. It had felt safer to keep my distance from my parents, from my younger sister, from all sorts of things. I'd never even considered the idea that they might be worried about me.

One Sunday, after you finally won me over, we took our one-year-old child to visit my old home. My parents met us at the front door, neither saying a word as they stared at me and you and the baby. My mother's eyes went wide and began to spill tears. Already regretting my decision to visit, I felt myself tense up, and I went to hide in your shadow so she wouldn't hug me. I didn't have to see my sister, as she was apparently renting an apartment close to where she worked.

"We're so glad she met a nice man, and now she's blessed with a child, too. I could tell she's happy the moment I saw her. It's like a dream. Isn't it, honey?"

"Yes… It's…quite a surprise."

"Thank you. I'm so happy to hear that you feel that way. Before we arrived I was prepared to be yelled at," you said with an earnest voice, lowering your head in a deep bow.

My mother had latched onto the baby and was showing no signs of letting go. I wondered to myself whether they'd act the same if they discovered we didn't know who his real father was.

Before long we were all drinking beer around a large box of delivered sushi, and I didn't really suffer the stabbing feeling I'd always felt in that kind of setting at home, the sense of feeling out of place, as though the air had turned into sandpaper. Maybe it was because of the toddler moving around among the adults.

"That went well, right? They're really nice people," you said on the train home, giving me a wistful smile. You were probably remembering what my Dad had said earlier: "We have a grandchild now, and a son at that. Isn't that great, honey? Finally another male!" He'd said this as you poured him a beer. You'd lost your own parents when you were young, so the words etched themselves into your heart.

After that day you would sometimes ask that we visit them again. On our second trip my parents called my younger sister and her fiancé to join us. My sister, always fickle in love since her youth, split up with that mild-mannered man, then brought along a new fiancé soon after that only to break it off with him as well just a few months later. It worried my mother.

When we visited my folks I would think of everyone as your family and just tell myself I was there with you. It was easier on me that way, allowing me to act more naturally. And the truth was that when you were there, sharing a lively dinner with my parents and sister, you blended in like you'd been doing it your whole life. Anyone would have thought that you were all actually related. I'd find myself smiling as I watched you enjoy yourself, and it wasn't too horrible even when the others poured me beer or expressed an interest in helping with the baby.

After several visits where we stayed over after drinking into the night, we got into the habit of visiting twice a month on a Saturday and staying the night.

And so several years passed.

After that, everything began to fall apart.

I'd reached the end of the third notebook. The writing filled the book to the last page, leaving hardly any blank space. I felt like I'd been left suspended, a side-effect of having read it all in one sitting. I pressed my elbows into the cover of the closed notebook and raked my fingers through my hair. I downed the last of my coffee, disregarding the fact that it was cold and streaked with cream.

The question had continuously haunted my thoughts the whole time I'd been reading: Was the baby me? My real mother was a serial killer, my real father a passerby that had paid her for sex… The thought made me feel like goosebumps were breaking out all over my skin.

I had no real proof, of course. It was just the thought that came to me based on the story so far. It was possible I was completely off the mark. Perhaps the child had somehow been disposed of long ago, as had been implied in the lines I'd skimmed at the very end.

Having read that far, however, I had grown even more confident that the man she called "you" was Dad. His close relationship with the author's parents matched that between Dad and my maternal grandparents. Having lost his own parents when he was young, the bond between Dad and my mother's parents were stronger than if they were blood relations. I didn't remember anything about my grandparents' place in Maebashi, but it seemed likely that this was the "home" the narrator referred to in the story.

Whatever the case, I knew I'd never last a week without reading the rest. I tried to come up with a way to sneak into Dad's study mid-week, but I couldn't think of a workable scheme. I'd need Yohei's help, even if only for an excuse to lure Dad from the house.

That thought caused me to start and I glanced at my watch. I realized I was already running late for meeting up with Yohei. I hurriedly thrust the notebook into my bag and rushed out of the coffee shop.

I hadn't even realized that it was long past sunset. I sprinted down the interchange station escalators and slipped between the closing doors of the Kyoto-bound train just fifteen minutes before eight o'clock, our appointed meeting time. I emailed Yohei to tell him I'd be twenty minutes late. As I stood there holding onto a hanging strap and gazing out at the twinkling city lights, rambling thoughts of the notebooks flooded my mind once more. Unable to arrive at a logical deduction, my thoughts went in circles, asking the question I'd already asked myself hundreds of times: Which of my two mothers was the author?

The author had written about a younger sister, but Mom

was an only child. Considered on its own, that point meant she couldn't be the author. That thought provided little comfort, though. I wondered if I was just too scared to come to terms with the idea that my real mother had killed people before having me and writing the notebooks.

The train was fairly crowded. Groups of housewives lost in gossip, a toddler sucking lollipops leaving a mess around her mouth, a young couple still at the awkward stage—it all felt diluted, like everyone was buzzing away as though they were in some separate, distant world.

An image like a scene from an old film came to mind: a woman, one of my two mothers (I couldn't tell which), living a strangely solitary life with the man in the notebooks, with Dad. Their life was quiet but their days were highly charged with powerful emotions that spiked with each shared glance…

I felt suddenly uncomfortable, realizing I had at some point begun to overlap their experiences with my own with Chie. The picking off of the beggarweed seeds, the timorous first consummation of love—my chest tightened as the events in the notebooks started to feel like something that had occurred between Chie and myself. I had no idea why it was happening, but I was appalled at myself.

And so several years passed.

After that, everything began to fall apart.

Those last two lines of the third notebook. I wondered how on earth their life together had gone to pieces. And I wondered whether they (and whether Chie and I) had only been so purely happy because our relationships were fated to collapse someday.

9

Yohei was angry, despite the email I'd sent telling him I would be late. It was the same barely-a-grade-up-from-a-diner steakhouse we'd visited a couple of days earlier, and it wasn't until Yohei had polished off all the meat on his plate, plus half of mine, and finally a black fig tart that he finally smiled, belching as he patted his stomach.

"Y'know, it's hard for anyone to stay grumpy on a full stomach."

A little alcohol had helped put me at ease as well. I ordered two coffees to stop us getting any tipsier, then handed Yohei the notebook I'd taken from the house. He spent a little while reading bits of text here and there.

"It's gotta be a novel, right?" he said, giving it back.

I felt completely deflated by how easily he'd dismissed it. "Hey, at least give it a little more serious consideration, as a favor to me if nothing else."

"Huh? I just read it. It's basically a love story about a prostitute."

"All right, then show me proof it's fictional. Proof."

"There isn't any proof. It's just obvious when you read it."

"Read it? All you did was glance at a few pages. I read three of these notebooks, cover to cover, and I checked to see how the last one ends. That's how I'm able to tell you it's real."

"Wow. So what did it say at the end?"

I recited the lines from memory, but they didn't seem to pique Yohei's interest.

"The way I see it, if you'd read them in a restaurant like this, tipsy and having eaten your fill of steak, you wouldn't have thought the contents real either."

I was about to object, but Yohei cut in with an "Anyways" and continued. He could be a real pain in the ass when he wanted. "Look at what actually happened. You're alone in an empty house, you find a closet door, usually shut, left slightly ajar. We're already in horror-movie territory. Then you go and find a cardboard box in the closet that's full of old stuff, including a women's handbag that looks like it might be meaningful, and a bundle of hair, then these notebooks at the very bottom. So yeah, in a situation like that, I'm pretty sure I'd have concluded they were a serial killer's confession, just like you did."

He had a point, but it was too late to agree and back down. "So what are you getting at? If different situations make us reach different conclusions, how can we know which is right?"

"I'm just saying that conclusions made in strange situations are usually wrong."

I knew his point wouldn't hold up against a logical argument, but I still found myself lost for an answer. Feeling increasingly agitated, I clammed up.

"Oh come on, Ryo, no need to pull that face. Geez, you're impossible. Here I was enjoying myself, but man, you really sober a guy up. All right, fine, I'll take it seriously from now on, we'll hypothesize that everything in those notebooks is actually fact. Okay?"

He looked at me and nodded a few times, making himself look like he was the elder brother. Knowing I'd need his help again I quelled my misgivings and outlined the contents of the three notebooks in as much detail as possible. Our waitress had an air of reprimand when she came over to refill our coffees, clearly annoyed at how long we'd been lingering, but I ignored her and carried on.

"Hmm," Yohei said after I'd finished and rubbed his chin, pulling on a beard he didn't have. "While we're doing this, I'll go ahead and assume your other theory that Mom was replaced by someone else is also true."

"Okay."

"We'll need to make a distinction. The one before you went into the hospital is Mom X. We'll get mixed up otherwise."

I nodded. Yohei had said it lightly but I knew it hurt him to talk about our Mom in this way, while he was still grieving for her. I was inwardly sorry for making him do so.

"From what you're saying, it sounds like you're pretty certain about two things: that the narrator is either Mom or Mom X, and that the man she talks about is Dad."

"Yes."

"Okay, let's suppose those things are also true."

"Everything's a supposition with you."

"Well, it has to be. We can't move forwards otherwise, can we?"

"Fine, fine."

"So based on these assumptions, broadly speaking, we need to work out whether or not you're the baby and which of the two Moms wrote the notebooks. Correct?"

"Well, pretty much."

"And just to double check, we're not fully certain the narrator really was 22 years old when the two of them met?"

"That's right. She wasn't sure of her age, so she used the year she was born when she answered him."

"Right, well, I guess that happens to me sometimes, like I'll just blank out for a second and forget how old I am. You said they had five years between them?"

"That's what the man said in the text, so it's probably correct."

"A five-year age gap fits with Mom and Dad in reality. Let's see… Mom got married when she was 24, and you were born a half-year later."

"Yeah, a textbook shotgun wedding."

Running it all through his mind, Yohei rubbed his chin some more. Then he slowly opened his mouth. "Well, okay, I think Mom was probably the one who wrote the notebooks."

"Wh-What? Where'd that come from?"

"That's the result of my analysis based on the information you gave me."

"What analysis?"

"All right. Dad was 29 when he married Mom. That was recorded in the family register, and it's something we both know. Now, the notebooks mention Dad registering his marriage to this woman. If the narrator had been Mom X, that would mean Dad registered two marriages in the space of just two or three years, first to Mom X, then to Mom. Plus, both would be shotgun weddings. That seems pretty tough to believe, although I can't be certain without going through the details of the old family register from before the move."

"Hmm."

"It's more likely that the reference in the notebook is the only time Dad registered a marriage. Working from that it follows that it's Mom who wrote them, because we know she married Dad. So I think she was probably wrong about being 22 when they met. She was either 24 or just about to turn 24 when they got married."

It was so simple, yet I'd missed it. Yohei had spent a year retaking his university entrance exams, and now he was repeating a year of school. There was no guarantee he'd even graduate, but he was still an engineering major and had the mind of a scientist.

"Following that line of thought the logical conclusion is that you were the baby, Ryo. Again, this is something to check in the old family register. If by chance there was another baby apart from you, the birth registration would be recorded there, even if the kid had died."

As his older brother I was rendered speechless. Yohei tilted his head and squinted a little.

"Of course, if Mom wrote it, the bit about her having a little sister doesn't fit because Mom was an only child."

As much as that made him look dejected, I felt myself revive. "R-Right? See, it's not as simple as you were saying. Besides, if Mom is the author, how do you explain the fact that she was switched with someone else?"

"Aah, right, that." His listless tone was getting on my nerves. "Well, I do have a hypothesis on that, and I think there's a good chance it's on the mark."

"Out with it, then. What's your hypothesis?"

"It's just a theory, so try not to get too worked up when you hear it."

"Enough melodrama, just say it."

"Well, you insist the switch actually happened, so the only way to deal with that is to say Mom X was your mother before you were hospitalized. But that was only for a short period. So basically, there were in fact two switches. Mom X switched places with Mom and pretended to be her for a few months or at most a year up until your hospitalization. You were so young that you didn't remember the first switch."

"Wait. Hang on. So you're saying that Mom wrote the notebooks? That she disappeared a few months before I turned four and that Mom X came to live with us instead? That I then went into the hospital, and by the time I was out, Mom X was gone and Mom was back again?"

"Yeah, that's it. It makes sense, doesn't it?"

"So who the hell was Mom X, this person who was only there for a few months?"

"Must have been Dad's mistress. 'And so several years passed. After that, everything began to fall apart.' That's what it said, right? Everything 'fell apart' because a mistress appeared. You can imagine the tragic scene, Mom thinking her life was over, like you saw when you skimmed through the final passage. Mom ran away, heartbroken, leaving only the notebooks behind."

"I wonder..."

"Then you got ill and some other stuff happened and Dad's relationship with this other woman broke down. He thought he'd driven Mom away for good, but they rekindled their romance. That sort of thing happens all the time."

I desperately looked for any chinks in Yohei's theory. Everything slotted together so neatly that, on the contrary, it rang false.

"What about the hair? It looked like something taken from a corpse."

"Probably Mom's from when she was younger. Maybe she'd left it with the notebooks, so Dad still had it when she went away. Maybe she was going to kill herself. Didn't it say, 'You won't let me live, you will kill me' at the end? Basically she was saying, 'I will die by my own hand, but you were the one who actually killed me.'"

I had to admit it was consistent. Too consistent.

"What about the time Mom was holding the pillow, watching me sleep?"

"Maybe she couldn't forgive you for growing attached to Dad's mistress, even if it was only temporary. When you got back from the hospital and saw her you blurted out something like, 'You're not my Mom,' right?"

"But the pillow incident was ten years later."

"She'd probably forgotten it for the most part, but it's possible she had occasional fits of anger that were directed at Dad and you. The bitterness would have been made all the worse, a hundred times worse, by how much she loved you. Since she was already a killer, maybe she couldn't stop her blood boiling, from wanting to just send you into the afterlife…"

My younger brother peered up at me through the shadow of his overgrown bangs, regarding me like he might a stuffed coelacanth specimen.

"And you're okay with this, Yohei? You can accept the idea that Mom killed so many people."

Yohei cackled loudly, exposing his canines and causing creases under his eyes despite his youth. "Come off it, Ryo. They're just theories, like I said. And all the presuppositions for said theories just a bunch of totally unrealistic theories themselves. Still, what do you think? It takes each premise you stated and seamlessly brings them all together. Hell, it's even pretty realistic. Impressive, even if I do say so myself."

"Yeah, except the glaring inconsistency about Mom having a sister," I said, trying to throw cold water on his self-satisfaction, but he seemed unfazed.

"Well, Ryo, maybe she really did have a sister."

"Mom did?"

"The notebooks say her sister had a fiancé, right?"

"Not just one, a good number of them. Seems she was a bit fickle."

"So maybe she went and did something that disgraced the family, and her father disowned her before she married."

"That's just another hypothesis."

"I do have a basis for this one, sort of."

"What is it?"

"Well, it's actually to do with Gran…"

"Oh, speaking of, how was she today?" I should have asked the moment I saw him, but it had completely slipped my mind, despite how kind she'd been to me back when she was in better health. I felt ashamed for having become so cold-hearted and selfish.

"Lost some more weight, I think. But she's doing better than I expected. And she got through most of dinner."

"You did good. I'll make sure to visit her soon."

"Me, too. Best to go as many times as possible, while we

still can. So, back to what I was saying. Do you remember Gran ever calling Mom by a strange name?"

I was momentarily lost as to what he was asking, but I soon remembered something that had happened a year earlier.

"Actually, I do. Something like that happened one time I was visiting her with Mom. I think it was… Emiko? Gran was crying and then she said, 'Emiko, is that you? Emiko, are you here?'"

"Right, that's it, just the same as when I was there. Mom looked really bothered and she tried to tell Gran her name was Misako, but Gran clung to her hand, crying and saying 'Emiko' over and over. There were other times like that."

"So, what you're saying is…"

"That Emiko might be the name of Mom's sister."

It seemed highly probable. Gran was always getting me and Yohei mixed up. Once again I found myself in awe of my brother's perceptiveness.

Just then, I had my own flash of insight. "This mistress you were talking about, Mom X. Do you think it's possible she could have been Mom's sister?"

"S-Stop looking so scary, okay? I'll say it again: it's just a theory. Hypothesis, conjecture, don't forget that. As a hypothesis though? Sure, it's possible. If anything, it seems pretty damn likely."

10

The next day, a Monday, we were fortunate to have bright, pleasant weather. On days like this there was always a tendency for the dog run to get too densely-packed with dogs, so I made an effort to pull myself together and focus on work. But each time I remembered how far off next Sunday was I grew irritable and felt like snapping at the dogs prowling around me.

It was bearable only because Yohei was due to visit Maebashi City Hall the next day to pick up a copy of our old, closed family register. Checking the registers was the only way to answer the questions I had about the baby in the notebooks, the existence of the author's sister, and about whether Dad—unlikely as it seemed—had ever been divorced. It would take too long to order the copies by post and there was a chance they wouldn't arrive by Sunday, when I was planning to continue reading the notebooks. I needed the information before then.

Luckily Yohei liked to do odd things and had jumped at the chance to help. The cost was nothing to sneeze at—transportation, including a bullet-train ticket, meal expenses, plus payment for his labor—but at this point that seemed unavoidable.

With all these thoughts racing through my mind I kept snapping back to reality only to find that I had stopped working, which set me on edge, fearing the sharp-eyed Ms. Hosoya might question me. She approached me before lunch, when the store had quieted down a little, and said there was something she wanted to talk to me about after we'd closed up for the day.

I had a bad feeling. I wondered if she might be planning to quit. It seemed inevitable. Her pay was low, and everyone got her to do work they considered unpleasant or difficult. It wasn't that Nachi, myself, or the rest of the staff were particularly lazy, just that she always managed to take out the garbage or clean the bathrooms before anyone else even noticed, and now everyone took such things for granted.

It had been the same when, half a year earlier, a medium-sized dog had been left, wounded, outside the cafe. The animal had likely been hit by a car. It was lying in a cardboard box, still breathing, even though its head was cracked open and one of its front legs was mangled from the shoulder down. I panicked and a part-time girl had to crouch down to keep herself from fainting. It was Nachi's day off, and I doubt he would have been much use even if he'd been there. Ms. Hosoya, on the other hand, had picked up the blood-soaked box, put it in the cafe's van, and driven away. I could have stopped her and done it myself but just looked on helplessly, standing rooted to the spot. I apologized when she got back, but she just smiled her usual smile, and washing her hands told me it was no problem. I never asked how she'd dealt with it. As her boss, as a man, I felt terribly ashamed for being so gutless.

In any case, her leaving would mean the end for the cafe. Of that I was certain.

It was a long afternoon. The dog run was packed and the cafe was almost at capacity, making it difficult to navigate between the tables without stepping on one of the tails lying here and there across the floor. And of course, Nachi had chosen today of all days to ask Ms. Hosoya to wash dog vomit off his work apron. I pulled him aside to quietly scold him. I told him he needed to wash his own things, asking what he'd do if Ms. Hosoya up and quit because he'd pushed his luck too far.

"She won't quit, trust me," he replied nonchalantly.

"How can you be so sure?"

"Because she's got a crush on you."

"What?"

"She was quick to land that kiss on your cheek, in the middle of that chaos when Cujo knocked her over. You've gotta hand it to her, she's good."

It was an odd thing to say, though it made me briefly recall her exposed chest and the sensation of her lips landing for mere seconds on my cheek after I helped her up.

"That was just from the momentum."

"She did it on purpose," he said with finality, folding his arms as if to tell me to give it up. Anyone looking on would have had a hard time telling who was scolding whom.

I was too scandalized to think of a response and could only stare fixedly at Nachi's face—a face I should have long since become familiar with. Staring at him with such intensity I noticed that he resembled a cat. His jaw was small considering his large frame, his eyebrows were thin, and his gently slanted eyes were admittedly lovely. Perhaps those eyes (or maybe the fact everyone assumed he was the cafe owner) were the reason why he was more popular with our customers than myself or Ms. Hosoya. As far as Shaggy Head was concerned, it was clear that he was indispensable. I wondered if that meant that I was the least prominent and the most worthless of us.

Just as my thoughts were turning masochistic a thin voice called out, "Here we are!" I caught sight of a silver-haired elderly lady tottering into the cafe. She had a cane in one hand and the other held a black pug that resembled a shoddily-made purse. It was Clutch.

Practically racing over to the old lady, Nachi guided her to a table, took her cane, set it against a table, and pulled out a chair; he then proceeded to give her shoulders a light massage. It was his usual routine yet I couldn't help but be impressed. He would give the best male escort a run for his money, and he was entirely guileless about it. The elderly lady came in almost every other day, bringing this dog that could hardly walk, and even as she said, "He's just happy to see the other dogs," I knew she was really here for Nachi.

He knelt on the floor and tapped Clutch on the nose, and the dog rolled his eyes around to look at him. The dog pushed out a surprisingly long, red tongue, licking the tip of his nose where Nachi's finger had been, but still appeared to be disinterested in nibbling the finger of anyone but his mistress. Nachi looked disappointed.

"Do you want to try holding him?" the old lady asked.

"What? Can I? Really?"

"I'm sure he won't mind, if it's you."

After this back-and-forth went on for a while longer the

little pug sat snugly within Nachi's hands held clasped before his chest. The dog, which must have weighed less than a pound, looked so tiny in Nachi's hands that it seemed like a miracle that it was alive, that its heart and lungs were working. Nachi's expression was one of earnest concentration, a look I'd never seen on him before. Even though Ms. Hosoya was out back still hard at work cleaning vomit from his apron, I couldn't help but smile as I watched him with the dog.

On the other hand there was a reckless part of me that didn't mind if someone quit, or if we lost customers, or even if the cafe went belly-up; a part of me that would accept it as inevitable. It felt like there was almost nothing left of the drive I'd once had to keep the cafe going no matter how hard I had to toil for it.

Contrary to my fears, Ms. Hosoya began to speak of something entirely out of left field. Half the lights in the cafe were shut off, and we sat facing each other on opposing sides of one of the tables.

"I want you to stay calm when you hear this. It's about Chie."

It came without warning. She had caught me totally off-guard. All I could do was stare.

"I think I've worked out most of what happened."

I continued to stare stupidly.

"To tell the truth, I've been visiting Okayama on my days off, several times now. I met up with Chie's parents."

"But...the address wasn't on her resume."

"No, it wasn't. The first thing I did was try the technical school she said she graduated from."

Knowing the office wouldn't give out their graduates' personal information, she had loitered around the main entrance and called out to students walking by. She was ignored by several but managed to catch the attention of a kind-looking girl. She gave the girl Chie's full name, telling her Chie had been engaged to her son but was now missing, and that he was trying to find her. She said she wanted to know if Chie had really graduated from that school seven years ago and asked the girl for her help. The girl had promptly taken an interest and made a number of calls to her seniors, their friends, and their circle of friends beyond that, and had finally managed to confirm that a girl with Chie's name was indeed on the list of graduates for that year. She even managed to get Chie's address from that time.

"I still couldn't be sure that the girl in the graduate list was really Chie. It was possible she had been using someone else's name. When I went to the address, though, it was clear the couple there was Chie's parents. I showed them my business card from the cafe, hoping to get them to relax, and introduced myself as a colleague of Chie's. I told them I'd borrowed a large sum of money from Chie and was looking for her so I could repay her. It was a weak excuse but they believed it. They didn't seem suspicious at all."

At that point my head was crammed so full of questions that I felt I was on the verge of losing control. "Wh-Why…" I didn't know where to start.

"It would appear that she has gone back to her husband."

"Husband?"

"She was already married. I didn't believe it at first, but her parents showed me photos from the wedding. Her husband owns the construction company she worked for right after graduation. Her parents said he had just taken over the business from his father, that he was young but already doing quite well for himself by the time they were engaged. It didn't last long, though. It turned out he hid the fact that the business was starting to fail. He also had a gambling addiction and bet on anything from bike races to horses. Of course, Chie didn't know any of this when they wed."

"Where is she now?"

"Her husband rents an apartment in Osaka. She's with him."

"Where in Osaka?"

"They wouldn't say. They wanted me to leave her be. They said they'd take the money for her if I really wanted to pay her back."

"This is ridiculous. I have to see her, talk to her, for any of this to make sense. Why did she hide all this? Why did she suddenly go back to him?"

"I asked the same of her parents. They refused to tell me on the grounds that it's a family matter. I persisted in asking why, but they only said that the situation couldn't be helped and that an outsider wouldn't understand the circumstances anyways."

We fell silent, with nothing to do but look at each other. The shock was so great it didn't register as real.

"Ms. Hosoya, why did you—"

"I'm sorry for being so meddlesome."

"That's not what I meant."

"The cafe's in trouble if you don't get back the money you gave her, right? If that's the case then I had to do something.

I don't want to lose my job here. This job suits me, and surely you know how hard it is to get a new one at my age."

I found it hard to believe she'd tracked down Chie's family merely for her own selfish reasons, but I chose not to argue the point. I wasn't the only one suffering due to Chie's disappearance. That realization came as a great comfort.

On the day I'd put up a help wanted poster before Shaggy Head opened, Ms. Hosoya had been the only one to respond right away. She and Chie had seemed to get along famously right from the time the three of us had sat down for an informal interview. A divorcée, the way Ms. Hosoya handled herself gave the impression that she'd overcome hardships during the course of her life. I imagined she might have a daughter, possibly around Chie's age. I didn't know if she had died or they'd become estranged, but I had wondered if Ms. Hosoya hadn't projected her feelings for her daughter onto Chie.

There was one event in particular that happened a few months before Chie vanished that led me to suspect Ms. Hosoya's maternal feelings. Chie had bent over a table to deliver some drinks only to have a man grope her jeans-clad backside. The offender was a middle-aged man with a Shih Tzu. I had come out to loudly protest his actions when Ms. Hosoya appeared with a bucket of water and, without a word, without even a twitch of her eyebrows, dumped it over his head. I had been genuinely surprised. Yet her attachment to Chie was evident even without such a demonstration. It was evident in casual everyday gestures like the way she would redo Chie's hair when it came loose, or rub anti-itch cream on her hands and feet when she had insect bites.

"Thank you. Really. You did well in finding them." My head dipped in a heartfelt bow. I felt wretched for having merely wallowed in my grief, for not having come up with a well-laid plan of action like she had.

"But the most important bit, Chie's whereabouts—"

"I'll go and talk to her parents." I had to convince them to tell me where Chie was, whatever it took. If possible, I wanted to rush to Okayama right there and then.

"That's a bad idea." The rebuff came without pause. She must have anticipated I'd say something like that. "Boss, you have to think. Think how upsetting it would be for them if another man turned up now. It would just toughen their resolve not to speak."

"But—"

"Don't be hasty. I'm not going to give up after one try, don't worry. I plan on going again and again, and I'll make sure they tell us what's going on, even if I only get a little info at a time. So for now, boss, you need to throw yourself into running the cafe."

It must have been hard for Ms. Hosoya to watch, to see how witless and spineless I'd become after Chie's disappearance. She must have been devastated herself, yet she had worked hard to keep Shaggy Head running in Chie's absence. I found myself too embarrassed to look her in the eye.

"Sorry."

At the moment, all I could do was apologize. My only choice was to leave it in her hands.

I didn't want to admit it, but it was possible that Chie had fallen back in love with her husband after seeing him again, that she had just dumped me. That I could believe. What I couldn't believe was that she had only gotten close to me in order to steal my money.

There had always been a part of Chie that seemed unknowable, and that was an aspect to which I was powerfully attracted. But ever since she'd left, I had begun to question whether she'd loved me as much as I'd loved her.

Maybe she hadn't, but I still continued to wish for her return.

11

Knowing that when it rains it pours, I was on the verge of panicking.

Even so, the next day I mustered all my energy and threw myself into work. It helped that the cafe was still busy, but the greatest incentive had come from Ms. Hosoya's warning that I really needed to concentrate on the business. I kept a keen eye on the interior of the shop, wiping stains from table legs where dogs had peed a little to mark territory, and making sure to run over with a damp cloth whenever someone got dribbled on by another customer's dog. I deftly handled female customers who tried to hang around and gossip at the register despite a line forming behind them, and even gave Nachi some headache pills when he was moaning about a hangover.

Of course, the whole time, no matter what I was doing, there was always some part of my mind that was thinking about Chie. I wanted Ms. Hosoya to get back to Okayama as soon as possible to ask her parents for the rest of the story, but she thought it would only backfire to be too hasty, while giving them plenty of time would help Chie's parents open up to her.

She finally decided she'd visit them again the following

week, but that felt like an eon away. It was the same for Chie's story as it was with the remainder of the notebooks—I didn't feel like I could endure the agony of waiting.

When it was getting towards evening, Yohei called my cell. I had been worrying over whether he'd managed to pick up the copy of the family register but I hadn't tried calling. I was only just getting back on track at work and knew that if something knocked me off-kilter I'd never regain my footing. I was scheduled to meet him that night, so I'd told myself to be patient until then. Yet the moment I took the call, all that patience proved worthless and I was utterly derailed from anything work-related.

"Ryo, I'm gonna stay the night," was the first thing out of the brat's mouth.

"Huh? Hey, did you get the register? And what do you mean, 'stay the night'? What about our meeting?"

Luckily everyone else had already taken their afternoon break except me, so I signaled the part-time girl next to me with a look and, still holding the phone to my ear, went up-stairs.

"Don't worry, I got it. I'll fax it from the hotel. I realized that there's no need to meet up if it's just to hand the register over. Since I've come all this way I'd like to see a bit of Tokyo. Forget about the steak dinner, could you spot the hotel in-stead?"

"Hotel? Ugh, you…"

He was right about faxing being more convenient than meeting up, but it still felt like I'd been cheated. In truth I'd wanted to see him as planned. I had all sorts of questions and complaints that I wanted to put to his scientific mind.

Yohei paused for a moment, perhaps intuiting the state of my own, and casually dropped a bomb. "To cut to the chase, Mom did have a younger sister after all."

"What?"

"But it seems she's gone."

"Gone? You mean, she went missing? You can get that from the family register?"

"The register says a court declared her missing, presumed dead. Have a look when you get the fax."

"What the hell? When was this? What year?"

"Let's see... She was declared missing in 1997."

"What? But that's well after the move to Komagawa. I was in middle school, and you were in elementary school."

"That's when the decision was handed down, but obviously she would have gone missing a long time before that."

"Yohei, do you understand how big a deal that is? It means the notebooks are real. The sister, she was killed."

"I knew you'd say that. Look at the register all you want, have a ball with all your wild theories. I'll join you for dinner again once you've cooled off." His tone made it painfully obvious that he wanted to hang up.

"Wait, hey, was there anything else you found out?"

"Everything else was in the clear. Dad was never divorced, and there were only records for us, no mysterious birth or death certificates for other kids. That's it for now."

That's it? I threw the phone onto the bed and thumped down on the rumpled sheets. But I got back onto my feet straightaway and started to pace the small room. It didn't calm me down in the slightest. I looked out the window and saw the dogs playing tranquilly as usual, ranging about inside the fence. They looked resigned and satisfied, seeming at once to behave like a pack yet also not like one at all. They each acted according to their own desires while actually conforming to subtle constraints of order. After watching them for a while I felt myself cool down a little, as I always did. I wondered if dogs actually exuded something that had a tranquilizing effect on humans.

I sat on the chair at my desk and switched on my laptop. Breaks were fixed at just fifteen minutes, but I wanted to do a little research into how courts declared people missing after hearing what Yohei had said.

It was after eight when the fax of the family registers came through. Unable to wait any longer, I was sitting at a table in the cafe, eating frozen rice pilaf I'd heated up in the microwave. I usually ate on the second floor, but the fax machine was downstairs so I had little choice.

Yohei had faxed the old family registers for both Dad and Granddad, documents that were rendered obsolete after the family's permanent residence was registered in Komagawa.

Although family registers don't have much text, they are hard to read, especially those from before everything was digitized. I neglected my food as I spent a long time skimming through the papers, but I finally managed to pin down a number of facts.

First: Dad's register was transferred from Sendai, in Miyagi Prefecture, to Maebashi when I was four and in the hospital. Neither Yohei nor I had visited, but Sendai was Dad's birthplace, and he had continued to live there with his unwed aunt after his parents had died. After the fire he had moved to Maebashi to live with my grandparents. There he had not only applied for local residency—moving from somewhere in Tokyo—but had switched his permanent residence from the Miyagi address at the same time. Even though he would again change his permanent address to Komagawa just a few months later.

Mom's name was there, listed as his wife, and the eldest daughter of her parents. She was in the Miyagi register because of the marriage, and nothing else, not her birthday or the date of the marriage, seemed to contradict anything I already knew. It was as Yohei had said. Apart from the fact that Dad had re-registered at Komagawa so quickly, there was nothing that stood out as particularly suspect.

The problem was with my grandfather's register. There, after Misako, Mom's name, was listed another name: Emiko, the second daughter.

I couldn't take my eyes off it. Emiko. The name Gran had let slip through tears in the nursing home. It was an obsolete register so each name had a diagonal strike-through. The name Emiko was struck off as well, but unlike the others, there was a strange inscription in the documentation column next to it.

> Presumed deceased March 10 1995
> Legal declaration August 5 1997
> Reported August 7
> Ryosuke Yanagihara (Father)
> Stricken from register

The note was written without punctuation. The name,

Ryosuke Yanagihara, was that of my late grandfather. Even though I'd been warned on the phone, actually seeing it with my own eyes gave me an icy shock that crawled up from deep within my gut. The night silence of the empty cafe felt suddenly oppressive.

Emiko Yanagihara.

Was she my real mother?

Had I lived my whole life not knowing a single thing about her, of her very existence, of this person who was presumed dead, who had left me behind? If she was the murderer who had written the notebooks, that meant the blood of a killer ran through my veins.

I sat in a daze. My head swirled with all the words and the various scenes in the notebooks. After a while they resolved together into a single floating image of a woman in a floral dress, holding a folded parasol and a white handbag. Her features were indistinct, but I could feel an incredible tenderness in the way she smiled in my direction. She looked like she wanted to say something to me.

Why had she gone missing?

From some internet research I'd done earlier that day, I'd gathered that if someone had been missing for over seven years, a relative could apply in court for a missing persons declaration, which effectively made the missing person recognized as deceased. It was too late to change anything, but I wanted at least to know what had happened to Emiko Yanagihara, how she had died. I would have to come to terms with it all, no matter how sinful the blood I'd inherited. The thought made me want to cry.

Dad's old register had been struck off in 1988, the time

of the move to Komagawa, but the other of the two obsolete registers from Maebashi, Granddad's, hadn't been struck off until 1998—a whole decade later. He had come with us to Komagawa, so why hadn't he processed his register at the same time?

There was only one answer: to sever Emiko's name from the family. With a missing person declaration to confirm death, her name would be absent from any new records made thereafter. So he'd waited, moving the register to Komagawa once that was done. They'd all been in it together; my grandparents, Dad, Misako. It was the only possible conclusion.

My eyes fell closed. I pressed my hands into my temples.

Holding still in that pose I could nearly make out a faint something, a silhouette peeking up from beneath my dark doubts. Maybe I didn't need to work out what had happened after all. Maybe the truth was already out in the open, and the only problem was that I just couldn't accept it.

Sometime later I picked up my spoon and finished what was left of the pilaf I'd heated earlier. Having cooled so much, it felt as tough as uncooked grains of rice.

12

Nothing particularly interesting happened over the next few days. Finding myself with no choice but to wait, I took each day as it came, my mental state in chaos as I felt both preoccupied and absent-minded. I did a pretty decent job at work, or at least I think so. Or perhaps it was thanks to the work that I was able to hold on. And besides, I got to work with dogs. If I made eye contact they came up to me, drooling a little. When I fussed over them, petting their heads or tugging at their ears, I found it impossible to dwell on other things. It's hard to gauge just how much those moments rescued me.

The hardest time was after the cafe was closed. At night, by myself, my head would fill with a never-ending stream of rambling thoughts. My feelings swayed between resentment that had nowhere to go and misery that made my chest clench. My thoughts kept running over the same things even though I knew it was pointless.

I would slowly sip a beer each night. I knew it would be better to snap out of it, to listen to some music or give Yohei a call, but for some reason I didn't want to. I preferred to sit quietly in my chair, a prisoner to the cycle of my thoughts. When the alcohol had seeped into my body, I would fall into

bed without even changing out of my clothes and be pulled
into a light sleep.

One such night, I felt a presence appear next to me, as
though someone was right there. It was my mother, at my bedside, watching me like she had watched "you" all those years
ago, staying with him until he fell asleep. The thought coiled
around me as I lay there half-asleep. I could almost feel her
pleasantly cool palm nearly touching my forehead. My young
mother, my mother who had died so young, whose name was
Emiko.

I tried to concentrate to get a better look at her indistinct
features, but instead countless words from the notebooks
rushed out, hiding her face from sight. She seemed to be calling out to me from behind those words. She was probably
long dead, and yet it felt like she was asking for my help.

Mother.

I tried to call out but my voice didn't work. I tried to move
but my body only twitched, like I was stuck in a fit of sleep pa-
ralysis. I was beset with helpless panic, but I maintained my
focus and at last a dim figure began to take shape against my
closed eyelids. The sleeveless summer dress, the white handbag, the face smiling in my direction—only for some reason,
it was Chie. Her almond eyes, her slightly creased eyelids,
the tiny mole underneath one eye, the girl I would never forget, no matter how hard I tried, her familiar scent, like spring
flowers.

I suddenly couldn't tell if it was my mother or Chie that
was calling for help. I knew I would probably fail them both,
let both of them die. That premonition swelled relentlessly.

My throat rasped as I groaned in horror, the sound of my

own voice rousing me. Sweating and gasping for air I began to sob quietly, the possibility hitting me that, just like my mother, Chie might already be dead.

Despite everything, Sunday eventually came around. I stayed at work as long as I could but ended up having to leave during the day's busiest period. I felt all the worse when no one seemed annoyed in the slightest, not Ms. Hosoya, not even Nachi, who usually liked to mouth off.

As before, I kept watch for Dad from inside the coffee shop next to the station. This time I was working by myself as it would be suspicious for Yohei to visit Gran two weeks in a row. It would be dangerous to spend too long in Dad's study, because unlike the previous week, I would have no way of finding out if Dad decided to cut his visit short and come back early. I supposed I would have to return notebook three and take number four, which I hadn't read yet. I could do that in less than five minutes.

It had been only a week, but when Dad appeared beyond the window he seemed to have lost even more weight. His shirt looked too baggy, the fabric billowing oddly. Yet still his posture was upright, and he walked with long strides. I followed his retreating back with my gaze until he was gone, surprised as I was by my own unbearably complex emotions.

I left the shop five minutes later and hurried to the house.

I stood in front of the open closet, not knowing what to do.

The notebooks were gone.

I had turned the contents of the cardboard box inside

out in my search but couldn't find either the manila envelope with the notebooks nor that handbag.

Had Dad noticed what I'd done? I tried to work out what I should do, but no bright ideas came to mind. Despite knowing it would be pointless, I looked through another box nearby, then another and another, until finally I had pulled every last box from the closet. The closet on the other side was all but jammed shut by the bookshelf, so it was very hard work getting it open. I dug through it all, finding nothing but old clothes, cutlery, and other useless things that made me feel fed up with the whole ordeal. There was no sign of the bag or the notebooks.

By the time there was nowhere left to stand in the cramped study, I had no choice but to give up. It took a long time to put all the boxes back and run a vacuum cleaner over the dust-covered room. I couldn't get everything back as it had been, so Dad would realize the boxes had been moved the moment he opened the closet. I no longer cared.

I went downstairs and sat at the kitchen table with a beer as I waited for Dad. It was the time of year when the days were long, but it was already getting dark outside.

It was after seven when Dad got back.

"Ah, you're here." He pulled a can of beer from the fridge, greeting me as usual.

"Were you expecting me?" I asked.

"I guess so." He drank about half of the beer at once, clearly relishing it before putting the can down. "It was hot today."

"How are you feeling?"

"Stop asking the same damn thing."

I'd known he would say that, but I'd seen how his wrist

had thinned down to the bone and ended up asking anyway. I had asked the question even though I knew the answer couldn't be good.

"Sorry."

"No need to apologize."

"Dad."

"Yeah?"

"Where did you put the notebooks?"

His expression remained unchanged. It was calm enough to make me wonder, for a moment, if he hadn't heard. He seemed not to notice the way I was staring as he picked up his beer can, drained it, and let out a sigh. Only after that did he look in my direction, though he seemed to focus on a point in the air between us.

"You've got one, don't you."

"Yes. But I just have to read the rest. I've only got the fourth one left now."

It felt like we were just chatting normally.

"I thought maybe you'd just taken one at random. Okay, so you've already read the first three."

I nodded.

"I took them out because I didn't want you to read them. I wanted to get rid of them while I still have the energy."

"Well, I've started now. I have to read to the end."

I pulled the third notebook from my shoulder bag and put it on the table. Dad was silent. He didn't even look at the notebook. He was looking at me with an unfocused gaze. The expression was oddly similar to Yohei's when he was sulking.

"Yeah, I suppose so," Dad said simply, after a long moment had passed. He got up from his chair and walked into the living room, right off the kitchen. He opened a drawer in the small bureau with Mom's—Misako's—memorial photograph on top, and pulled out the manila envelope. I didn't know what his real motive was, if he'd hidden it there deliberately right by her photo. When he came back he handed the envelope to me and said, "Sorry, but I'm going to go upstairs and get a little rest while you're reading. It's rather pathetic, but I'm a lot weaker now so even walking a bit takes a toll. Call me when you're done."

It was unusual to hear Dad complain like that, but instead of offering sympathy, I only managed a vague response. Listening to the steps creak as he climbed the stairs, I pulled out the contents of the envelope. Even though I finally had the notebook in my hands I felt extremely anxious, as though it might be snatched away at any moment. I hastily put the three I'd read to one side, then picked up the fourth. I took a deep breath to try and calm down, but it had little effect.

I knew the last lines of the third notebook so well I could easily recite them:

And so several years passed.
After that, everything began to fall apart.

My hand trembled as I flipped through the pages, thinking that what I was about to read described how things fell apart, as well as the events that led up to my mother's death. For a moment the desire to read it nearly faltered, but there wasn't any turning back.

One afternoon I was out walking along the street, my son's hand in mine, when someone called out to me using my maiden name.

"Wow, whatta surprise! Long time no see! Gosh, I was pretty sure I had the wrong person, but I thought I'd try calling out anyway. You look so different. I wonder what it is. Your face? It's like you're a different person."

The man was balding, making it seem like he had two horns. He was a contractor from my old workplace. His prices had been reasonable and he came quickly when we called, so we'd used him for most of the office supplies. I was usually the one to place orders.

"Oh, so you got married. Hey there, young man. You look like a good boy. How old are you?"

My son fidgeted shyly, then held up his fingers to show the man his age.

"Wow, that's great. What's your name?"

The man with the horns had given me a garish scarf one Christmas. He said it was a present, so I'd thanked him and taken it, but after that I couldn't bring myself to order supplies as usual. It was one of the many reasons I was eventually forced to leave the company.

"Hey, this kind of thing doesn't happen too often, let's go get some tea. Gosh, this sure is a surprise. I guess women change this much when they get married. I want to ask you all about that. 'Cause, you see, I'm still a lonely old bachelor!"

I could see inside his gaping mouth when he laughed. "I can't, sorry. I've actually got some errands to run."

"Oh come on, I saw you just strolling along. I could see you from way over there. Look, I'm in the middle of work myself, but you've got to cherish this kind of coincidence. How about it, young man? Wanna get some juice? Or maybe ice cream?"

"We really can't. We have to go now."

But the man kept on speaking, acting like he hadn't heard me. "You quit real sudden. That was pretty mean, even if it was a long time ago. Hey, that reminds me, did you see it in the papers? A little while after you left, someone was murdered there, in your company's office. Hmm? Oh, so you don't know. It was about four, maybe five years back. And the guy that got killed was someone we both knew pretty well. Can you guess who it was?" he said, prefacing the name of the man I had killed. "And what's worse, the killer clubbed him to death with one of my garbage bins. Talk about leaving a bad taste in the mouth. You know, the kind everyone used, steel, looked like an umbrella stand. One of those."

I hiccupped as I felt my heart tighten like a clenched fist. All the shading of the scenery around me dried up, everything suddenly appearing like the set of a play that glittered with hostility. I felt like the insides of everything I could see around me had been broken the whole time. All Nan-Core gone. I was hit by the intense realization that this was how the world had always looked to me, long ago, before I met you.

"H-Hey, what's wrong? Huh? What—are you okay? You're very pale."

I couldn't reply, sure that my voice would sound strange.

"Hey, your kid, you're hurting him. Hey, your hand!"

I noticed the crying voice and let go of my son's hand. I'd been squeezing too hard. I immediately took hold again and started to walk away.

"Hey, wait, wait! You're acting mighty strange." He grabbed my shoulder, enough to make me nearly lose my footing. "Are you running away? Why the rush… Cat got your tongue or something?

Hey… Do you actually know what happened? Were you… Were you involved in some way?"

He was peering at me, his expression like a distorted mask.

"No. It's just a shock, that's all," I said over my shoulder, shaking free of the horned man's grip and briskly walking away. My son started to cry again as I dragged him after me. The fake scenery of the city creaked and jostled around his high-pitched bawling, sounding as though the set pieces might shatter apart at any moment. I would never escape. But I had no idea what to do.

About half a month ago two police detectives came to the house while we were in the middle of dinner. One was a heavy-set man around 50, the other a younger man with thin eyebrows. When you opened the door to greet them they showed their badges and gave their names, and after confirming your name they told you in a courteous tone that they would like to ask some questions of your wife. I didn't want them in the house and rushed to the door, but you had already let them inside.

"We're very sorry to interrupt your dinner. This won't take up too much of your time."

When they were seated in front of the low table in the next room, the older detective retrieved a notebook from his pocket and read out the name of the horned man. He then asked me to confirm the date, time, and place I had seen him. More than a month had already passed since then so I had assumed that everything would be okay. I could hear you on the other side of the closed room partition, reading a book or something to our son so he wouldn't make a fuss.

"Now then, please understand that this is just procedure, we have to confirm details whenever someone calls a report, you see. I have to say though, it was quite a headache finding this place, what with your last name changing when you got married, and then moving house."

The detective laughed, rubbing the back of his neck. From beginning to end he was the only one who spoke. The younger detective just sat there, never saying a word.

"Well, uh, according to the man who made the report, you, ma'am, appeared to know something important about a case from sometime back."

The detective continued, outlining the details of the case, reading off the name of the man who had been killed, the whole time watching me with eyes that seemed fossilized, isolated somehow from the shifting expressions of his face.

"So, ma'am, you knew the victim, is that right?"

"He was a superior of mine at the company I used to work for." My voice didn't waver. I mentally scolded myself that I couldn't get distressed like before.

"According to our records, uhm... You started work there about seven years ago, and you were there for a year or so."

"Yes." I didn't really remember, but I supposed their records were correct.

"At the time, did you have any kind of, umm, personal relationship with the victim? Outside of work, I mean," he asked, whispering to show he was aware of your presence in the other room.

"No."

"How about after you left? Did you meet him at all, maybe just once?"

"No."

"And the murder. Did you know about it?"

"The first time I heard about it was when I saw that man."

"I see, I see." He kept writing in his notebook. The other detective was staring at me. "And what did you think when you heard about it?"

"I was shocked."

"I see."

"He said it so abruptly, not to mention right in front of my son."

"Right. It's just that, well, the man told us that you were acting abnormally. He said you turned very pale and looked like you were on the verge of having a fit."

"I was in shock and I wanted to get away from him as quickly as I could. He kept asking me to go for a drink."

"Oh, did he now."

"I refused, telling him I was in a hurry, but he wouldn't listen. He used to say all sorts of things to me before, too, at the office."

The detective fell silent and frowned, then wrote something in his notebook and snapped it shut. I thought he might say he needed to take my prints, just in case. But I was sure I had at least cleaned them from the garbage bin and the door handle.

"Well, we're sorry to have taken up your time. I think we've got all we need, this should be fine." After putting on his shoes the overweight detective turned around, looking cramped in the small doorway. "The case is already five years old, and we pretty much exhausted every line of inquiry then, so it's not often anything new comes up. It's a real pain, I tell you. Again, our apologies for the disturbance."

I didn't feel like eating after the detectives had left, so I cleaned up dinner while you gave our son his usual bath.

"So, that issue from earlier. Did you have anything to do with it?" you asked me later when we were lying in bed together. "I had wondered if you were the way you used to be back then because you were trying to atone for some sin. I think I asked you if that was what it was."

You'd asked me when we met: *You're trying to make up for doing something bad, that's why you're a prostitute?* I remembered it well.

"Was it for the case that those detectives were asking about? Was it atonement for that?"

"No. I didn't have anything to do with that murder."

"Well, why didn't you tell me? That you'd bumped into the man who reported you."

"I didn't think it was worth mentioning. Then I just forgot about it."

"And you're not lying?"

"I'm not lying."

"All right."

You reached out and took my hand under the bedspread, eyes fixed on the ceiling. Your lips were pressed tight, like you were holding in check a flow of words, leaving them unspoken as you pushed them back into your heart. After a while you turned to face me and whispered in a strained voice, "I… I haven't forgotten. The fact that I killed the boy is a part of me now, something I'll never forget. I actually think about him even more now that I'm happy." You fell silent, seeming to consider what you'd just said. You were silent for a long time, but just as I thought you were falling asleep, you whispered, "From now on, if anything even a little strange happens, I want you to let me know. We're husband and wife now."

Then you said goodnight and let go of my hand.

I had lied to you, and because of that a small fissure had appeared some place out of sight. Everything around me began to leak through that crack and the air grew thinner by the day, by the week.

Nothing changed in the way you acted, though. You still called out to me when you returned home every evening, and you still pulled your tie loose with your free hand the moment you stepped through the door. You seemed as carefree as always when, earlier this evening, you taught our son to do a somersault, tumbling around with him after his bath. It was enough to make me wonder if nothing had really changed, that perhaps you hadn't noticed the transformation in the air. In bed, however, you held me like I was a child again but left the calling of my body unanswered. You haven't answered it for a long time now—even though I thought the fissure might be stopped up if, once again, we could meld into each other within that feeling that was like a living death.

Was it punishment? Did you know that I'd lied?

I'm writing at this late hour because I can't sleep. I decided to write down the whole truth that I didn't tell you after the detectives came, like for Mitsuko's memory all those years ago.

Just because I've managed to write everything down doesn't mean I'll have the courage to let you read them once I'm done. But now that I've started I can't stop, and I scribble like someone possessed whenever I'm alone, night or day.

Yet even now as I write this, the fissure creaks and groans and continues to widen. I can feel it quite keenly. I have to stop it somehow, I must. If I don't stop it soon the fissure will become like the pitch-black well from Michiru's garden. No, maybe it's already transformed, maybe it's just waiting for the right moment to swallow me up head-first.

If you'd pressed for an answer back when you'd just become you, I probably would have told you the truth of everything I'd done without thinking too deeply about it. How many people I killed, how I killed them, how it felt—all of it. I could still talk to you like that, in the beginning. I could even have killed you. It was probably because I'd lost the ability to kill you that I stopped being able to tell you such things.

Why was that? Because I had no reason to kill you. Because, living with you, I was haunted by the feeling that we were slowly, ever so slowly, dying together. The stronger this sensation of dying became, the more I perceived happiness bursting out around us, the world vibrantly alive. Nan-Core—for a long time I didn't think much about it because it was so naturally abundant around me that I didn't have to think about it.

It was in your voice when you talked about fate, in the blue stone in the keepsake ring that you gave to me, it was in our secret kisses at night, in the tiny beggarweed seeds, it was everywhere, always there. I don't know why. It was just that kind of time. And during those years my surroundings were alight with magic, the kind of which I'd never seen before.

And it was my lie that had broken the magic.

But that doesn't make sense.

I'd done something terrible to you once, a long time ago, before I met you; something so terrible, this lie was nothing in comparison. That time the young boy got his neck trapped and died.

Surely that was by far the greater sin?

I'm confused. I get all mixed up every time I try to think about things in earnest. Back in that park I condemned you to hell. There's no mistaking that. But the same act became a catalyst, turning you into you. If the events of the park had never taken place you wouldn't have borne the burden of guilt, and you wouldn't have become so deeply involved with a dirty whore... Am I right?

Oh, what should I have done? Supposing I had to first put you through hell in order to meet you. If everything was predestined, did I have no choice in the matter? Was everything already decided the instant that gust of wind snatched away the little boy's sister's hat in the park? Is it totally acceptable that we met only to suffer afterwards? Did we find each other only to fall apart, as some form of punishment for my sins?

The thought of being locked up in a tiny cell for months or years, just waiting for the death penalty, is so terrifying it's enough to drive me insane. A burning pain sears my chest, like I'm suffocating.

I don't know why I suddenly thought of the death penalty. This strange pain in my chest... I wonder if it's guilt, the kind you told me about. Has your suffering conscience finally spread to me too?

I just fell asleep on this half-written page, for about an hour. It's almost dawn now. I had a strange dream. I was looking for snails to drop into the dark well, like I used to. But I wasn't in Michiru's big garden, with the trees and the pond. I was in something like a solitary cell, locked up, waiting for my execution. But that well was there, in a corner next to one of the walls, and each day in that cramped space I had nothing to do but think about the well. I needed a lot of snails, and luckily, the cell's damp stone walls had some large ones clinging to them. On that particular day, however, I was finding it hard to catch one—they were either out of reach or slipping away at the last moment. I felt the pull of the bottomless abyss latch onto me. I was starting to feel numb, only just able to breathe, when one of the snails fell off the wall. I hurriedly reached out my hands. It was our son that I caught, curled up and small like a snail. He looked up at me and smiled. *Oh, thank goodness. I'll be okay if I drop a snail this special into the dark well. I'll be free.* Those were my thoughts as I smiled back.

For the last few days I've been imagining this one thing, over and over again. I have no choice but to ask this of you. It would be so wonderful if you were to do for me what I did for Mitsuko. Right now it feels like this is what I have always desired, ever since I thought of you as "you" for the first time.

You could do it any way you want. Killing me is the only way to save me from falling alone into the dark well. I'm sure I'd be surrounded by joy, by a sparkling brightness, as my consciousness drifted further and further away. I would become a memory inside you. Then nothing would scare me at all.

I know it's a hopeless wish. Helping me that way would make you a murderer. I would be forcing you to suffer an even greater burden of guilt.

It's nearly time for you to wake up. You'll brew some coffee and make breakfast as usual. It's okay, I'm calmer now. Or emptied out, maybe, like an abandoned husk. I'm not sure what it is that abandoned me. This flat version of myself has become a part of a world that's nothing but warped stage scenery.

When I read over what I've written, it feels like someone else's writing. It's a weird feeling. Did the fissure not really exist at all? I find I'm less and less certain of whether that fissure was there or not, of whether anything changed.

I can't shake last night's dream from my mind. Everything around me is in ruin, but the dream of the special snail is the one thing that's still bright and vivid. So I can't help myself from wondering what might happen if I really killed him. I don't know why, but I feel like my wishes might be granted if I repeat what happened in the dream. Is it possible that I could change fate by sacrificing the most important thing between you and me?

Why do I keep having these thoughts, even though I know such things would cause you great pain? Something is wrong. I know that much. And I don't believe that dreams carry messages. Even so, the more I think about it, the less I'm able to stop myself. Michiru, Mitsuko, Ramen, the boy that died in the park have all come together, calling out to our son. Their voices calling out *join us, join us* are growing louder within me and my body feels like it's about to burst open.

I don't think I really understand what it is to feel grief. Perhaps that's why I am capable of doing things that make you suffer.

Ah, but unless I do something terrible enough to destroy everything I won't be able to break free of this place.

A mother who kills her own child shouldn't be allowed to live. Even in the depths of despair I'm sure you would feel the same. If I were to beg you then, you would surely kill me yourself. You would grant me this wish. You wouldn't need to feel any guilt at all for killing the woman who murdered your son.

It's a risk I have to take.

As long as it results in the fissure being sealed shut, I'm ready to do anything. I can't be sure it's there, but a fissure is still a fissure. Whether it exists or not it's right here, right inside my throbbing, aching head, and it's linked directly to the dark well.

I'm sorry. I'm so sorry. I can't stop myself.

I'll make sure he doesn't suffer when he dies.

I'm trying to think of a way. Our son came out of me, he appeared through me—does that mean he's mine? He's not yours, not in any real way. Nobody knows who the real father is, he's just some loser. His mother's a killer. Yes, he inherited bad blood. Better if he dies.

This is the last of my notebooks. I won't write anymore. You will read this in a few days after everything is done and I am no longer alive. I know this, because I don't have the courage to let you read this while I live.

You won't let me live.

You killing me is my only salvation.

Because you are my you—

Please, don't ever forget that.

But if some enchantment, like that which I felt when you spoke of fate, were to bring me back, and you were to take me in your arms again, I would like to have another child. It would be your true child, one that will take the place of this child that I am going to kill.

That is my wish.

At the top of the stairs I saw that the door to the study was open. Dad was lying on the tatami mats, using a folded cushion as a pillow, his back to me. I thought he was asleep, but when I stood outside the door he asked me in a low voice, "Did you finish it?"

"Yes." I walked in and sat beside him. "Should I grab you a blanket?" I asked, trying to be kind, but he didn't respond. He rolled over wearily and ended up on his back, staring at the ceiling.

"If you reached the end, you must already have a pretty good grasp of things."

"In my own way."

"Well then, that makes this easier. Go on. You can ask whatever you want."

He was deathly pale. I didn't want to talk about any of it. I wanted, if possible, to make him rice porridge or something, get him to eat, then rest properly. At the same time I had the overwhelming feeling that if I didn't talk about it then I'd never have another chance.

"The one who wrote them is my birth mother."

"That's right."

"And someone really did switch places with her. You, Mom, even Gran and Granddad—you were all in it together, you lied to me when I was a kid."

"Yes, that's true."

"My real mother's name is Emiko."

Dad pulled his eyes away from the ceiling and looked at me properly for the first time that day. "Where did you get that name?"

"I got copies of the old family registers from the city hall in Maebashi. They said that someone by that name went missing. But the truth is that the whole family conspired together, and then killed her."

I saw Dad's emaciated body twitch. He stared at me with wide-open eyes that he didn't try to avert. Slowly, he turned his head to face me as well, then closed his eyes. "Not exactly. Emiko didn't give birth to you, Ryosuke. It was Misako. So it was Misako who wrote the notebooks."

"What? But Mom…"

"By 'Mom,' I assume you mean your recently-departed mother. The truth is that she was Emiko. She was the younger sister of Misako, your birth mother." Dad paused for a moment, letting that sink into my brain. His eyes were still closed. "Ever since we all moved to Komagawa, since the day you were hospitalized, Emiko falsified her age and pretended to be Misako, her own elder sister."

"So the one who was killed was…"

"Misako."

The characters of the name written in faded ink on the threadbare sheet of Japanese paper floated up in my mind's eye—Misako. The lock of hair had belonged to my real mother, to the real Misako. So that was it.

The fog that had shrouded my thoughts was gradually lifting. After he told me, it felt like that had been the only possible answer. If I had gone one step further I would have realized the truth. Why hadn't I?

The thought came to me suddenly that my younger brother might have worked it out already. If he'd compared what he already knew with the information in the old register, it was possible he'd found his way to the same conclusion. And didn't that explain why he'd decided to stay in Tokyo, and why he hadn't been in touch since coming back? Maybe because he didn't want to talk about it he was actively avoiding me.

At some point Dad had opened his eyes, which were fixed on the ceiling again.

"Why did you have to kill her? Was it because she tried to kill me?"

Dad shook his head very slightly, almost like a denial, but he didn't answer. I gave up on the questions and silently waited. When Dad began to speak at last, his lips trembled, as though he had to force each word out.

13

The three of us, Misako, myself, and you, still a young child, were staying at her parents' house in Maebashi when it happened.

It was the middle of the night and I suddenly woke for some reason. The futon next to mine was empty. I wondered if Misako had taken you to the bathroom, but the sheets were cold to the touch. On top of which, there was an indistinct breeze in the air. I instinctively checked the wristwatch next to my pillow. It was nearly two in the morning.

When I got up to check I saw that the sliding screen leading to the corridor was open, as was the glass door facing the garden. The door had been unlocked and left several inches ajar. I tried calling Misako's name but there was no reply. It was a mild night in early July, and the garden was still and aglow with pale moonlight.

I could sense that something terrible had happened. I shoved my feet into the wooden garden clogs and quickly searched the grounds, checking out beyond the fence. Then I went back to the house to look through the other rooms. It was so late that the trains were no longer running and I didn't imagine Misako had taken you back to the apartment without me, but I called anyway for the sake of trying. After that, I woke Misako's parents.

My mother-in-law was distraught, insisting we call the police. I did my best to calm her down. I thought it would be faster if we searched ourselves, as I doubted the police would mount a proper search, not for a wife and child who happened to have left the house in the middle of the night. And truth be told, I was also concerned about those detectives who had come to question her. I was afraid that if she caused any trouble they might start treating her as a suspect.

I called Misako's younger sister Emiko instead, knowing she lived nearby. She had a car she could use. I gave her a quick summary of what had happened, apologizing for the late hour, and asked if she could go to our apartment, just in case. Misako hadn't answered when I tried calling, but there was still a slight chance that she had gone back there. Besides, if the worst happened and she got into some kind of accident, the apartment would be the first place anyone would call.

Emiko agreed without hesitation. She needed to come over and pick up a spare key, but it was late so she could still reach the Tokyo apartment in a little over an hour if she hurried.

My father-in-law and I split up in our search, while my mother-in-law stayed in the house. With an unspoken understanding, we headed towards the river, not the train station. You probably don't remember, but there was a branch of the Toné River just north of the house, dividing the residential area from a stretch of farmland. When we went on walks we usually went as far as the riverbank.

We continued our search upstream, my father-in-law on the south bank, while I crossed a bridge to look on the north side, checking the undergrowth and bushes and sometimes calling your names. I could hear the sound of the water burbling as the moonlight glinted and shattered on the river's surface. The leaves on the trees and ground shone as though they were coated in a film of mercury, and I had a clear view of my father-in-law jogging up and down the far bank. Despite this, I felt somehow that I wasn't seeing what I really needed to see, and it made me so anxious I felt like I was about to choke.

Time slipped away. After a while the concrete dike gave way to weeds which grew up from the side of the path, and it became harder to see to the bottom of the riverbank, but easier, from where I was, to see the riverbed on the opposite side, where my father-in-law was.

We followed a wide curve in the river and that was when I caught sight of a small figure standing a ways off on the opposite bank. A little boy in his pajamas, looking like he was about to step into the river at any moment.

"Over there!" I yelled towards my father-in-law, pointing from across the river. I broke into a run and saw him do the same out of the corner of my eye.

"Ryosuke!"

"It's dangerous! Stay out of the river!"

We were both calling out to you but I couldn't tell whether you could hear us. You were already ankle-deep in the water, looking like you were trying to cross the river.

"Ryosuke, don't move! Wait right there, I'm almost there!"

You looked over briefly but didn't show any signs of giving up. You took another step and in that instant you appeared to slip in an unexpected deep section and to be pulled into the water, re-surfacing quickly as you began to be carried downstream. I scrambled down the incline of the bank. Then I heard a splash as someone else jumped into the river farther upstream on my side. I was sure it was Misako. I assumed you'd been trying to reach her on the other side.

I kicked off my shoes and jumped into the water and immediately sank in up to my shoulders. The current was faster than I'd expected and I was rapidly swept further in, reaching a point where it was too deep to stand. We were on a bend in the river, and the bed near my side was deep where it had been eroded.

I struggled to swim against the current, but it was impossible to progress upstream. I craned my neck and looked around, doing what I could to avoid being swept downstream.

I saw Misako floating towards me. She had you in one arm, the other arm thrashing so as not to sink. I reached out to grab her but there was no way I could reach her. My hand barely grazed her as she passed by in a flash. I followed after her, summoning all the strength I had left. I was single-minded in my focus. Each time I tried to shout I swallowed water. Each time I thought my fingers touched her body, the distance between us would open up again.

The current weakened once we were clear of the bend. Misako had started to drift as though she'd given up, constantly dipping under the surface of the water, pulling you under as well. I finally caught up just as she was about to go under again, and managed to catch her from behind. Her eyes—your eyes too, you were still in her embrace—were wearily closed, and neither of you seemed to be breathing. My father-in-law was shouting something from the edge of the river. I struggled to pull you both in his direction, and eventually I managed to secure a foothold on the riverbed.

I lay the two of you onto the grassy bank and my father-in-law and I began emergency resuscitation. You'd only been in the water for something like three minutes, so I was sure you'd be okay. And thankfully you were quick to cough up the water and start breathing again. We needed to get you both into an ambulance as soon as we could, so my father-in-law decided to carry you and run to the nearest house to wake up the residents and ask to borrow a towel and use their phone. We didn't have mobiles in those days.

I stayed behind and tried to help Misako by continuing artificial respiration. She still had a pulse and was breathing, if weakly and in spasms, but she wasn't regaining consciousness. Her face was deathly pale. I wanted to warm her up but I had no means to do so. After about five minutes her breathing began to stabilize, so I stopped forcing air into her mouth.

It was then that I saw that her left wrist was sliced open. The cut was deep and ugly, like she'd made a number of incisions in the same place. Having been rinsed clean by the water the bleeding had stopped, revealing split flesh that looked inky black in the moonlight. I had no idea how much blood she might have lost before jumping into the river. I was terribly upset to see she that she had intended to die. I couldn't figure it out. All I could think was that it had something to do with the murder those detectives had mentioned. She'd been acting oddly ever since the questioning, and the whole incident had bothered me more than it should have.

But even so, I'd never thought she would do something like that.

I seriously considered whether the too-bright moonlight was the culprit, whether it had somehow driven her mad.

I realized she was looking at me, her eyes just slightly open. It was the same look she sometimes got when she was watching me—just observing. She was pale and expressionless and tears were streaming down her face, her eyes the only part of her that seemed alive. I knew then that she really had killed someone. But as she watched me like that after having failed to take her own life, I felt paralyzed, unable to speak a word. And even though my mind was still reeling, I knew one thing for sure. The sole reason she wanted to die was that she couldn't bear the thought of losing me.

Inexcusable, isn't it.

I still think so. If she'd tried to kill herself out of guilt for what she'd done, that would have been somewhat more justifiable. But that wasn't the sort of woman she was. It simply couldn't be helped. She'd always been strangely naive, or rather simple-minded, and she couldn't really grasp ideas like temperance or moderation. She was ill-formed that way, yet for some reason I couldn't help loving her.

As she continued to watch me I stared back, feeling like I might be sucked into her eyes, and suddenly I wanted to help her to die. I was seized with an odd sense of obligation to help her die, if this woman for whom living was so difficult yearned for me so. I would only have had to press down on her nose and mouth for a while. It would have been easy. I could tell my father-in-law that she'd drowned, that she hadn't started breathing again, and that would be it. I knew it would make her happy...

I didn't do it, of course. I massaged her cold body in silence, continuing until the paramedics arrived with a stretcher. I didn't say a word the entire time.

That was all that happened that night. You were both held at the hospital but in stable condition. I called our apartment from the hospital and told Emiko everything that had happened. It came as such a huge shock that she couldn't summon the strength to drive home, and she told me she'd stay the night. In truth, she had already started reading Misako's notebooks. Later on she told me she had found them in a stack on the table, placed there like a will. In light of the contents, she had decided not to say anything about them until the next day at the earliest, when things would be a little calmer.

Everything was frantic for the next few days. Just as I'd feared, the hospital got in touch with the police. They tried to interview

Misako, but she was no longer speaking. The doctor said it was probably stress-induced retrogressive mutism, not her just being willfully silent. My father-in-law and I told them what we had seen, as well as our supposition that Misako had gotten out of bed and that her son had wandered out after her, still half-asleep.

So listen carefully: Your mother had wanted to die alone. That much was clear. I know what she wrote in the notebooks, but even under all that stress, when she was wandering the borderline between sanity and madness, she didn't hesitate to choose to end her own life. She was never capable of killing you. She doted on you. It was almost painful to see how much she loved you.

The police told us to look after each other, but that was the end of their involvement. The detectives from earlier never showed up, they probably didn't even hear about it. You were discharged after a couple of days, but not Misako. It was a general hospital with a psychiatric department and the doctors wanted to keep her under supervision, so it took longer for them to release her.

Meanwhile, even though you'd been discharged, your condition started to deteriorate again. I took you in for a check-up after an extended fever had left you worn out, and was told you had pneumonia. Something nasty had found its way into your lungs from the river water. It apparently happens sometimes to people that have nearly drowned. The doctor said there was a chance of dangerous sequelae in such cases and gave me a letter of introduction so you could be admitted to a hospital in Tokyo that had a specialist on staff.

I couldn't take much time off work and was exhausted from having to shuttle between the office, your hospital, and Misako's hospital in Maebashi. I briefly spoke with my in-laws when we met at either of the hospitals or when we needed to talk on the phone, but I didn't have the time to sit down and discuss things properly. It was on a Sunday two days before Misako was due to be discharged when I finally managed to make time to visit the house in Maebashi. It was a hot and humid night, with thunder rolling in the air. Emiko was there, too, and that was where I was first shown the notebooks.

"Just read them," she said.

I cooped myself up in another room and went through them all in order.

I couldn't stop shaking. It was like the words on the page were twining themselves all around me. My head swam and I couldn't think. When I returned to the living room everyone had their eyes pinned to the ground—Misako's mother, her father, Emiko—and none of them dared to glance at me. I got the impression that they hadn't said anything or even moved for the entire two hours I'd spent reading the notebooks, as if they had hunkered down and turned into stone statues.

When Emiko finally opened her mouth to speak, the voice that emerged was a cracked falsetto, like she had to force it through a throat that was pinched tight.

"We can't let her stay with the child," she said.

Her parents remained utterly silent. I think they were all starting to come to that particular conclusion. They were just too afraid to come to terms with it, all three silently pondering their own convictions. Like I said to you just now, I don't believe, based on what I saw, that Misako actually tried to put you in harm's way. I can see that quite clearly now, but I was beside myself at the time, having just read the notebooks, and I fell under the illusion that she had actually tried to carry out what she'd written. I thought that she'd failed once but might one day try again, and actually succeed. Then there was the fact that she'd killed so many other people, and, more than anything, the truth of what happened in the park… I couldn't accept any of it.

"For a while, we weren't sure if we should let you read them. If it might be better for us to handle this by ourselves." My father-in-law was talking to me, but he still wouldn't look my way. "But that just wasn't possible. There is your son to think about. Whatever we end up doing, we need your help."

"What do you mean, 'whatever we end up doing'?" I retorted automatically, my head still numb.

"Under normal circumstances, we would try to get her to turn herself in. Don't think we didn't consider that."

My mother-in-law broke into tears. "But we can't, not that. How many times have I told you? She really will go mad if we do that."

Do you remember Misako mentioning in her notebooks her fear of being shut up in a confined space? She couldn't even ride elevators, you know. Maybe it was something like claustrophobia. She hated walking underground or taking the subway. It would have been the cruelest torture for her, being locked up for any prolonged amount of time. Emiko, her parents—they knew that all too well.

"If only she'd drowned, been carried away. Then we wouldn't have to…" There was a clap of thunder just as Emiko spoke, and we suddenly lost power. We sat for a while in the dark, unable to see each other's expressions, no one getting up to fetch a flashlight. "…We wouldn't have all had to get involved in this freakish situation. If she'd just died I wouldn't have had to tell you any of this, not you, not Mom, not Dad… I could have gotten rid of the damn notebooks without any of you knowing. She's a killer. She's not my sister anymore, not family, not anything."

Under the cover of darkness I couldn't see the expression on Emiko's face as she said all of this, but the more she spoke the more her voice began to sound bold and reckless.

It marked the beginning of what became a bizarre family discussion.

We all poured out our innermost thoughts, provoked by the darkness. It was hard to tell who we were talking to, or if we were all just talking to ourselves.

...how to make her take responsibility... we can't just do nothing... it's unforgivable... she'd just get the death penalty anyway... the poor girl... shouldn't we at least be the ones to do it... even just to see it through... we're the ones left... all those people Misako killed... we'll forever carry the burden of her crimes...

Our faces resembled white, expressionless masks floating in the dark. Even there I felt like my drowsiness might get the better of me as I hadn't slept properly for ages. I wanted to nod off, to not have to think or feel anything, to simply fade away. I recalled, as if it had all been a dream, all the times we had gathered around the same table to drink under bright lights.

I should have killed her when I'd helped her half-drowned body onto the bank. The thought wouldn't go away. She'd wanted it, her eyes had begged me to do it.

"Let's do it. It's the only thing we can do, Dad. It's for her own good."

I remember Emiko saying that.

The lights had come back on at some point.

"Right, then. And everyone's on board with this? No regrets?"

"No regrets? Of course we'll have regrets."

"Mom's right, Dad. There's no way to do this without regretting it."

When the women spoke, their voices were choked with tears.

"I guess so. So we'll make her pay for her sins in a manner that will leave us with as few regrets as possible. And you, do you accept this?"

I didn't realize right away that he was talking to me. At the same time, I was strangely cognizant of what he meant. I don't remember if I nodded. I think I probably did. If I hadn't, they wouldn't have done what they did.

On the day Misako was discharged from the hospital, her parents bundled her into the car and drove her away. She still couldn't speak. I was to stay behind to collect her things and pay the remaining bills. She watched me from behind the car window right to the end. The way she looked at me remains burned into my soul. Her eyes shone black yet were blind even as she tried desperately to see out.

When I went back to her room I lurched over the sink, throwing up bitter bile. I sat on the empty bed, telling myself it was for the best, that it was wrong for such a woman to be allowed to remain in this world. I tried hard to convince myself. I kept seeing the image of her, scrawny and filthy, that first night in the park when she had come up to me, asking the time. I knew I would never meet someone like that again, no matter how long I lived. And I knew that regardless of whom I met, regardless of how perfect they might be, I would never love anyone the way I loved that broken, malformed woman. I knew that to be true.

It goes without saying that I told them I wanted to do it myself if we were going to go through with it, because I knew that that was what Misako wanted.

Emiko lashed out furiously. "It can't be you. We're not trying to grant Misako her final wish. We're doing this to make a murderer pay for her crimes," she said in tears, practically clutching at me.

There was something unhinged about her bloodshot eyes. It didn't come as a surprise; she had found the notebooks in our apartment, then read through them even as she trembled in fear, all by herself on the night of the incident. She wasn't the only one acting strangely. You read them too, Ryosuke, I'm sure you understand. My mother- and father-in-law as well as myself, all four of us had read the notebooks. We all felt like someone had reached deep into our hearts and minds only to savagely tear things apart. The confessions had been otherworldly but strangely vivid, leaving us all disoriented.

They were the backdrop for the series of events that followed.

My father-in-law, usually a gentle person, was resolute during that time. "We'll take care of it. We're suited to the task, since we're old and don't have so much time left, and as her parents you have to let us see this through." Then he said, "Think of your son. You'll condemn him to suffering for the rest of his life if he ever learned that his father killed his own mother. That can't happen. We have to protect the innocent as best we can."

Still… I guess that's all just an excuse. Even if no one had stood in my way, I don't think I could have actually gone through with it. I could never have taken her last breath, not with these hands. Your mother was mad to ask such a thing of me. She had strangely overestimated me in that regard.

They told me about a small dam, a long way up the river, deep in the mountains. They used sleeping pills to put her to sleep. Then they blindfolded her, tied up her limbs, and let her sink to the bottom of the lake behind the dam. They tied rocks to her so her body wouldn't float back up. When my father-in-law told me all of this, he gave me her handbag and the lock of hair.

Maybe there's not much point in saying this now, but you should know that everyone agreed that we had to do everything in our power to protect you, as you were the most sinless of us all. Maybe we only managed to get through it all because we never lost sight of that one goal. It didn't make any difference whether you and I were related by blood or not.

Perhaps it was because I had lost my parents when I was so young, but I was determined to arrange things so you wouldn't have to feel the pain of losing even one of your parents, let alone both. I also wanted to make absolutely sure you never learned that your mother was a murderer. At some point, the idea of her younger sister Emiko taking Misako's place seemed to spring up naturally. I don't remember having asked formally, and I don't think anyone else came up with the idea.

There was one thing, however, that I had been dimly aware of for a while. I had a suspicion that Emiko kept jumping from one fiancé to the next because she had feelings for me that she couldn't bring herself to voice. I think that might have complicated things for her. She became increasingly unstable after what happened to Misako and started to experience violent mood swings. She might not have been conscious of it herself, but it was clear in the way her eyes clung to me that she wanted me to rescue her. It made sense that they were in fact sisters. When she looked at me that way I fell into the bizarre illusion that it was actually Misako watching me. That aside, I knew that no one else would be able to take on the role of being your mother in the same way Emiko could.

Consider that the four of us were, essentially, accomplices.

Myself, Emiko, and your grandparents would carry the same burden for the rest of our lives, and the most natural way for us all to raise you was for Emiko to become your mother. She would be more than that; she would actually become Misako. By engineering this we hoped to protect you from finding out who your real mother was, from finding out what happened to her.

Emiko wavered fiercely. On the one hand, she believed that abandoning everything she'd been to become your mother, to become Misako, would be recompense for what she'd done to her sister. On the other hand, she wondered if she was only thinking like that to justify being with me. She spent a long time troubling over it. In the end, however, she decided to be reborn as Misako. She decided to simply honor our original promise to protect the most innocent member of our family. I think she realized it was the only possible solution. She'd never reach a decision if she kept on worrying about it.

You were in the hospital longer than expected. After you finally recovered from pneumonia, various other complaints started popping up; your tonsils swelled up or your ears or nose got inflamed.

It was a stroke of luck, for us at least. We moved to where we didn't know a soul, and Emiko began her new life as Misako. They were sisters and had similar facial features. Emiko had also lost a lot of weight after what happened, and after she fixed her hairstyle the likeness to her elder sister was shocking. You didn't remember anything of what happened before you were hospitalized, even the fact that you'd almost drowned, so I hoped you wouldn't notice.

After some time we filed a missing person report with the police, saying Emiko had vanished. We included a photograph of Misako from the time when she was breastfeeding you, when she was slightly round-cheeked, and pretended it was Emiko. We chose a photo that least resembled either of them. We needn't even have done that in the end. The police don't do much when it comes to missing persons.

Sorry, but could we leave it at that for today? I've covered most of it and I'm too exhausted to continue. It's a shame this happened. I wanted you to only remember how kind Mom was. I can't explain it logically, but I think Misako was alive alongside Emiko the whole time. Don't you think so?

I made up a story about a fire in our old place and disposed of all of the old photos, but I kept hold of the handbag with her hair inside, and the notebooks. Sheesh. I really don't know why I did that. I'd pulled them out again so I could throw them away before I died, but I kept putting it off every day. And you went and found them. Maybe it's some twist of fate.

Dad really did look exhausted. His face was bluish black, practically corpse-like. Without saying a single word to comfort him I went downstairs and left the house.

My legs were shaking. I had already assumed my real mother was dead. But the shock of hearing Dad tell me what had happened was much more vivid than I'd expected. And I wasn't even related to Dad by blood—my real father was some unknown passerby, someone who had paid for my mother's body.

More than anything I felt like I'd been taken in. I finally knew the truth, but I didn't feel even a sliver of satisfaction. I don't know if I was angry. If I was, I think it was probably directed at myself, not at Dad or any of the others. I was angry that I was the only one who hadn't made a sacrifice, angry for having lived such a free and easy life, for being so ignorant, for failing to seek the truth.

I had been a small child at the time, nothing more. But a kid could still have done more for his mother, even if it amounted to nothing more than a weak protest. I should have screamed and cried like crazy to see her when I was in hospital. I shouldn't have let my memories from before the hospital slip away so easily. At the very least, I should have continued always to insist that she had been switched with someone else.

I hardly remember the route I took back to the station or even how I got back to the cafe. I only came back to myself when I stopped next to the window in my darkened room to look vaguely out across the dog run.

I couldn't shake the feeling that I had somehow abandoned my mother.

Without any dogs the land outside seemed barren and too wide, like the surface of a lake brimming with dark water. How did it feel to drown, blindfolded, with your arms and legs bound tightly? I could see my mother, writhing but unable to move, sinking down, bubbles spewing from her mouth. It felt like she would continue sinking inside me like that forever, as everything around her turned insubstantial, blurred.

Had she suffered badly? Or had she breathed her last without even knowing what was happening?

She was a murderer. It couldn't be helped.

The words suddenly sprang into my mind. I couldn't tell if they were mine. It felt like someone had whispered them into my ear. They were my words, of course. They were the words that came to me, mostly without resistance, each time I read in the papers about a condemned criminal being executed.

There was no other choice, they were killers. Killing killers wasn't murder.

My mother the killer. My mother, who had been bound hand and foot and thrown into a lake because she was a killer. Of my real father I knew nothing, not the way he looked, how he was raised, even whether or not he was alive—just that he was the kind of man who would hire a hooker. For a moment I could feel their blood melding inside me, seething. As I was alive by this blood, what did that make me?

I shuddered as a cold sensation crept from my knees to the small of my back. I felt for the first time the presence of something cavernous and dense nesting inside my heart, like an unfathomable darkness.

14

Tuesday, a couple of days later, Ms. Hosoya left to visit Chie's parents again. Shaggy Head was open all year round, closing only for the New Year and the *O-bon* holidays. The staff worked on a rotation to manage the six days they had off each month, and Tuesday was Ms. Hosoya's scheduled day off that week.

It had been hot and humid since morning, and the sky had threatened rain all day long. The cafe was mostly empty, even though a drop never fell. The few dogs pacing in the field seemed to lack their usual vigor. They couldn't take off their coats, and didn't do well in the humidity.

When the weather was like that the dogs gave off a musty, animal smell. Nachi kept pulling a face and complaining about the stench, throwing open the windows only to shut them again once all the cold air from the air-conditioning had dissipated. I actually liked the way it smelled for some reason, kind of like something scorched.

With nothing much to do it was hard to concentrate. I hadn't slept for a few nights and I had to bite back a number of wide-open yawns. I was hopeful for some new information on Chie, but my senses felt dulled as though the sluggish gray of the sky was hanging, leaden, within my skull.

After listening to what Dad had to say, I'd stopped caring about anything. I started to believe that Chie was beyond my reach, that she would never come back.

I mean, if she'd wanted to see me, she could have snuck away from her husband. The fact that she hadn't done so even once spoke clearly of her feelings. Even if Ms. Hosoya discovered Chie's whereabouts, there was nothing I could do as long as she didn't want to see me. Occasionally I caught myself thinking about Chie like she was already dead. Just like my mother. It was curious, as though I was losing the ability to grieve for them individually. They had, without my realizing it, merged into a single ache.

My heart wasn't in it but I made a show of working hard, and as I wiped down the tables and handed back change to customers, the hours eventually passed. When the cafe emptied out that evening I decided to take it as an opportunity to close up half an hour early. I'd never done that since the cafe opened.

After Nachi and the other girl working part-time had rushed home in glee, I filled a mug to the brim with coffee, but even after finishing it I just sat vacantly with my elbows resting on the table.

No matter how hard I tried to gloss over it, I always succumbed to an unbearable sense of emptiness when I was by myself. When night came and the quiet of the mountains eased its way into the building, even my sense of being seemed to dilute.

I nodded off a few times, with my head still propped up in my hands. It seemed like too much trouble to get up from the chair and go upstairs. I don't know how long I sat there.

I heard the roar of an engine climbing the hill, then a car coming to stop in front of the cafe. When I dragged myself over to open the front door I saw Ms. Hosoya, looking sharp in a suit, step out of a taxi. I was about to walk over when I saw someone take her outstretched hand and slide out of the vehicle. My heart was already telling me it was Chie, but it took my mind a full second to catch up. In that second I thought I was looking at my mother, still young as she walked through the park at night, her body bruised, haggard. That was how slight Chie appeared. Her cheekbones jutted out from her pale face and her neck was shockingly thin.

I couldn't process any of it. I moved on instinct alone. I ran to her side and held her softly like she was something that might easily break. That she had very nearly been broken was clear from a single glance.

"Chie…" My throat was choked up, and I could barely get my voice out.

She seemed like a doll. She didn't pull away, but she didn't return the embrace either. It was enough. Nothing else mattered so long as Chie was alive and I could hold her.

It took a long time before the doll opened its mouth and the words came slipping out. "I'm so sorry." Her voice was wretched, barely audible.

A pitiful woman—I didn't know what to do to put her at ease. I was almost suffocated by a rush of emotion. I held her a little tighter, just a little so she wouldn't be afraid. "D-Don't go away ever again," I stuttered and stumbled over my words. In the end, that was all I said.

I supported her as she hobbled step by step up the stairs

to the cafe's entrance. Ms. Hosoya was already busy inside, wearing an apron over her suit. In no time at all an omelette and salad were set on the table.

"This is all I can manage, but we need to get something in her stomach. And not just Chie. You look like you're ill yourself." She put a bowl of bread stewed in milk, like a sort of porridge, on the table next to Chie. "I hope this will be easy enough to get down."

Chie thanked her, her eyes still on the floor.

"Chie's got a bad cold, you can see she's still recovering."

I nodded absently. No cold could possibly have caused such a total transformation. I had lots of questions, but I knew it wasn't the time to ask them. Chie didn't have much of an appetite but she ate the milk porridge, blowing on it as she carried it to her mouth. As I watched her, I realized I didn't want to ask her anything about it, ever. I wanted to just let it lie.

As though she'd understood what I was thinking, Ms. Hosoya said, "We can talk about the difficult bits tomorrow. We should let her get some sleep for now, once she's finished. She should be okay here for tonight. Go on, boss, eat up."

I did as I was told and took a bite of omelette. The soft yolk seemed to melt on my tongue and I suddenly realized I was completely starving. I polished off the whole plate in the blink of an eye. On the way out Ms. Hosoya gave me a few paper bags with Chie's medicine, instructing me on how she needed to take them. The pills had been dispensed from a number of different hospitals and seemed to include anti-depressants and sleeping pills. I was shocked by the number of different types of drugs and started to feel uneasy. I had yet to absorb any of what was happening, but that didn't stop me from feeling a sudden and powerful hatred for Chie's husband.

15

The sky that had been on the verge of rain for so long finally opened up, and the next morning brought a heavy downpour. I went down early to the cafe and was making coffee when Ms. Hosoya arrived at seven, as we had agreed. She had taken the business car home the night before, and driving it back meant she had been able to stay dry.

Chie was still asleep on the second floor. She had woken in the middle of the night and started to shiver violently, telling me she wouldn't be able to get back to sleep, so I had given her one more of the sleeping pills and massaged her back. We didn't say much, only speaking when necessary. I was amazed to find that even after all that had happened, the natural ease we'd had around each other back when we were happy, when we could spend hours in companionable silence, hadn't faded.

"It was a surprise. I had never expected Chie to be there in person. I had a hard time convincing her parents. I all but dragged her away with me in the end. Chie herself hardly knows what she wants in the state she's in, as I'm sure you've noticed."

Ms. Hosoya's eyes were red and bloodshot behind her glasses. She had used her day off and driven in again early in the morning, so of course she was tired, but it didn't come through in the way she spoke. I was too filled with remorse to properly apologize to her.

Chie had been close to contracting pneumonia, and her doctor had told her she needed complete rest and quiet. Her husband had dropped her at her parents' home a week ago, and he was supposed to pick her up on Friday. That was in two days' time.

"For the time being we have to keep her hidden. He probably knows about the cafe."

Ms. Hosoya then told me the fragments of information she had gotten from Chie and her parents. Chie's husband's name was Tetsuji Shiomi. He had always enjoyed gambling and became increasingly obsessed with it after his company went under, so he was struggling financially. At the same time, he took to the bottle, getting drunk nearly every day, and beat Chie because she was the nearest thing at hand. It was the typical picture of someone on a downward spiral. It was so textbook that it was hard to believe it was real.

"They told me he'd been a decent, caring man before they got married. They'd trusted him. The change came the moment the ceremony was over. In time Chie was working hard to support the two of them, putting up with it, hoping that things would someday go back to normal. Even though he'd apparently used up all their money and broken her ribs and teeth from beating her."

Something bright white sparked across my frontal lobe. I was momentarily blinded, unable to hear Ms. Hosoya as she spoke. I had never really known what rage felt like until that moment. At the very least, I'd never felt such tremendous anger directed at a single human being before.

"Two years ago she ran away, unable to bear it anymore, taking with her what little funds she'd managed to stash away. She didn't tell her parents where she was going because she knew Shiomi would look for her. She said she had been overjoyed when she started working here after some time."

I remembered the somehow unstable expression she'd worn when she approached me, asking me to hire her. It was that odd sense of danger that had so thoroughly driven me to distraction.

"I think Chie became complacent. A year and a half had gone by without anything happening, so she decided it would be safe to call her parents. She hated to think they were worrying about her. She didn't give them an actual address but she did say she was fine and working in Nara, at a cafe with an area for dogs to run around in." Ms. Hosoya paused for a moment, sighing under her breath. That was the only time she let her guard down, a hint of tiredness rising to the surface. "I don't have all the details but it seems that Chie's parents' house was quite old, and they'd renovated it using some of Shiomi's money. Her mother also went through a period as a follower of some new cult I'd never heard of, again borrowing large amounts of money from Shiomi for donations. With such a history between them her parents were so indebted to him that they could barely look him in the eye. He visited them repeatedly, demanding his money back, always pushing for information on Chie. Eventually, they let slip about the call."

The full picture was slowly coming into view but I stayed

silent, listening intently to her voice so I didn't miss a single word.

"Chie hadn't given them the address, but there aren't many cafes in Nara that also have a dog run. Going through them one by one he'd track us down eventually."

She was right. When Chie was working outside, she was visible from any number of places around the cafe. The idea that Shiomi had once come close to Shaggy Head brought with it another dizzying rush of anger.

"She said he just turned up without warning. He was leaning against her apartment door one night when she got back from work. When he saw her he clung to her, desperately begging for help, telling her he'd be killed if he didn't pay the money back."

"So what?! That's no reason to leave without a word!" I half-shouted the words, briefly losing control.

Ms. Hosoya kept her eyes on me, remaining quiet for a while. When she opened her mouth again, she spoke more slowly. "Shiomi is under pressure from the yakuza. It's been going on for so long he's started acting like one himself. He knows all too well how to threaten Chie, how to hit her where she's most vulnerable."

I waited for her to continue but she didn't say anything else, so I prompted, "By vulnerable, you mean her parents?"

"There was that, too. He threatened to send the yakuza that were coming for him to her parents' home, telling her they owed him lots of money, that he'd get it back even if it meant causing them pain. Even worse was the fact that he'd worked out Chie was seeing you."

"Shit. He went that far?"

"I'm sure he threatened to harm you, telling her that anyone messing with another man's wife had to pay. I think it was the photos, though, that were probably the hardest for her to ignore."

"What photos?"

"I don't really know. Just that he'd threatened to send you some photos from her past, ones she wouldn't want you to see."

We both fell silent. Part of me felt that I didn't want to ask anything more, but still I had to know. "Did you find out about what work Chie did when she was living with Shiomi?"

"Not specifically. But I think the photos she didn't want you to see are probably related."

It wasn't hard to imagine the kind of photos they'd be. I felt ready to cry and wail aloud. I didn't want Ms. Hosoya to see how badly my lips were quivering. I envisioned untold numbers of men jacking off as they flicked through photos of Chie in various indecent positions.

"She had no choice but to become Shiomi's puppet, just as before. She couldn't refuse him when he told her to steal all that money from you. I don't have any details, but seeing how emaciated she is, there's no doubt he had her working hard to bring in more money."

"I'll kill him." The words leapt from my mouth, startling even myself. At the same time I felt a wave of something like rapture course through me.

Ms. Hosoya frowned, giving me a sharp look. "You can't think like that."

"What else can I do? Report it to the police?" Ms. Hosoya must have been well aware that reporting anything was only a stopgap solution, setting off a game of cat-and-mouse. "Whatever we do, the moment Shiomi finds out Chie is missing he'll be here to have words with me."

The decision came naturally, without conscious thought. I would lure Shiomi and then kill him. If I didn't, I was certain my anger would eat me alive. I hadn't been able to protect my mother, so I wanted to protect Chie no matter what happened.

"There's a chance he'll come right here. I got the impression that Shiomi was under a lot of pressure, too. So we have to be quick in moving Chie somewhere else."

What would the kind woman before me think, I wondered, if she found out I had the blood of a murderer running through my veins? The notion just popped into my mind.

When I imagined running a sharp blade through Shiomi's body, I felt a numb burst of something like elation. Right through the heart, with my own hands. I felt confident that I could do it. My blazing rage had already blasted away the hatred I'd felt for my own blood. I would never have supposed even moments earlier that I could come to terms with being my mother's son in such a manner. No doubt Dad would have said it was providence, fate. I couldn't help but feel it myself, the sense that everything happening was somehow predestined.

Had I thought about it rationally, I might have decided that blood had nothing to do with it at all. Maybe it wasn't just me, maybe everyone has a killer lying dormant within, waiting for the conditions necessary to rouse up and fall into place. How else were acts like genocide or war possible? I remembered reading in some book that senseless acts of killing increase during peacetime.

"At the very least, boss, we need to decide our plan of action. It won't be long before people start to arrive."

I looked at the clock on the wall. There was less than half an hour before the cafe opened at nine. Chie was probably awake by now. The lack of options meant I didn't have to waste any time pondering the decision. I hated to let Chie out of my sight, but the only recourse I had was to accept Ms. Hosoya's offer to take her in. The weather being the way it was, the cafe would be quiet. I asked her to take Chie back early that afternoon, then to take a few days off to stay with her and get some rest. We were discussing how to work out the workers' schedule for when she was away when Nachi turned up and called out, "Morning!"

While Ms. Hosoya bundled him off to one side and took him through the extra hours, I took Chie's breakfast up on a tray.

To my surprise, she was still sound asleep. I was suddenly anxious that the pills had been too strong, but her breathing was even and her expression placid. Her eyes were moving under her eyelids and her eyebrows were twitching. She was probably dreaming. A faint smile spread like a soft veil across her too-prominent cheekbones. It was as though she knew I was there, like she was smiling at me.

She was back, and that was enough. It didn't matter what had happened or what kind of work she'd been involved in. As I watched her, there was no doubt in my mind. She deserved my appreciation, if anything, for having made it through such exceptional hardship. My mother had been a prostitute, too. With that in mind, I couldn't help but find the word "fate" floating into my mind once again.

The rain showed no sign of letting up, even after lunch. On such days, only the more eccentric of our customers ventured out, usually regulars that knew each other and who liked to relax around a table for hours, gossiping or boasting about their pets. The dogs, used to the routine, stretched out lazily on the floor, as though the gloom and rain were too much for them to handle. They wagged their tails obligingly each time their masters broke into laughter.

The cafe was peaceful, salon-like. I spent the whole time thinking of how I was going to kill Shiomi.

My mother had stopped killing once she met Dad. But it was different for me. If I hadn't met Chie, I was sure I would have lived my whole life without taking another's, without the killer inside me ever waking up. This would be the first and last murder. By killing Shiomi, I was protecting Chie. I had to be reborn as someone worthy to be her partner, I had to be strong and filled with vigor, and I had to sever all links with the old, indecisive me. Killing Shiomi would serve as a rite of passage. Successfully pulling it off would prove once and for all that I'd accepted in the truest sense that I am my mother's son. So I had no choice but to kill him.

I had to avoid being caught once it was done, of course. Getting arrested would mean not being able to make Chie happy. For that reason I needed a little more time, enough to plan and prepare everything carefully. Shiomi wasn't sched-uled to collect Chie from her home in Okayama for two days, so I hoped to have at least that long.

This was, as it turned out, optimistic. Shiomi discovered

that Chie was no longer at home before the day was out, perhaps by calling her home or going over to check on her. He
called soon afterwards, a little after one p.m. Instead of the
cafe, however, he called Ms. Hosoya's cell phone. He'd probably gotten the number from Chie's parents. Her phone rare-
ly rang during work hours, and it was clear from the way her
eyes sharpened as soon as she brought the phone to her ear
that it was Shiomi.

"Yes, speaking." She threw a meaningful look in my di-
rection and went out onto the deck. Nachi was fussing over
Clutch, the black pug, and chatting to a group of customers.
He gave me a puzzled look but I ignored him and followed her
outside. "I'm afraid that's impossible... She's still ill... No...
That's none of your business."

I leaned over the handrail and looked around, not caring
that I was getting wet. Something told me he was nearby, but
I couldn't see anyone, just the gray of the trees getting pelted
by the rain. Ms. Hosoya was giving brief responses into the
phone. My clothes and hair were already damp from the gust-
ing wind as it carried a fine, mist-like rain that sprayed the
deck. I felt an unpleasant sweat springing up. I shifted my
weight back and forth, growing impatient. I wanted to snatch
the phone from her and talk to Shiomi directly. I wasn't sure I
could hold back the impulse much longer.

"How much do you want? ... No, that's too much... I
can only withdraw so much at a day's notice... Okay... Fine,
I'll tell him. And you'll hand over the negatives as well? ... I
will... And what time do you want me there?"

Their conversation ended abruptly. Ms. Hosoya stared at
the phone, dumbfounded, when she pulled it from her ear.

"Sounds like he's been driven into a corner. He said they'd kill him unless he repaid part of his debt immediately. He was so terrified he was barely coherent. I don't think he was putting on an act."

"What did he say about Chie?"

"He knows she's here. He wanted me to tell you he'd be here soon to sort things out with you. Right now he wants us to buy Chie's compromising photos plus the negatives. I'm surprised he's willing to part with those, actually. They would be a cash cow for him. It's probably a sign of how desperate he is for quick money."

"How much does he want?"

"He said three million yen. When I told him that was too much on such short notice, he said one million would do, for the first time, anyways. It sounded like he'd already heard from Chie that you had nothing left after the two million she took. I don't think he's the type to give up because of something like that, though. He made it clear that this would be just the first time, so we can assume he plans to wring you dry, perhaps hoping to make you borrow money from relatives, or a loan shark, even if you have to put up the cafe as collateral. It's by sheer chance that he doesn't have the luxury of time right now."

"A million."

"He wants the money tonight, at the lookout point at the top of the mountain road."

I felt so pathetic for not even having that much money. The only possibility was to borrow it from Dad. I felt bad, knowing I'd left without a word after he'd explained everything about my mother, but it wasn't the time to worry about such things. We would just about make the deadline if I called and asked him to wire the funds immediately. I was still busily running this through my mind when Ms. Hosoya spoke again, surprising me with what she said.

"Boss, Shiomi said he wanted me to bring the money, not you."

"He said that? Why you?"

She looked puzzled, but there wasn't a trace of fear in her expression. "He probably just wants it to be a woman, because we're not as strong as men. In their wedding photos, he looked shorter than Chie and seemed pretty unfit. And he's probably hoping I'll come up with the money if you can't."

Is that why he called her phone? What a fucking coward.

"Shit. Does he really think I'll just stand back and do whatever he says?" My rage was starting to boil over.

"Please stay calm. Right now our first priority is to get the negatives back, so we should play along for the time being. I shouldn't have any trouble getting a million yen together."

"I can't ask you to do that. I can borrow it from my father."

"In that case you can borrow it from him later to pay me back. We can't spare the time to explain the whole situation to your father, not at the moment."

"But that's—"

"It's unlikely Shiomi would offer the negatives for so little in any normal situation, but right now he's too panicked to consider the consequences, which could work out well for us. If you look at it that way this is an opportunity."

I didn't know what to say anymore. I'd dragged Ms. Hosoya so far into this mess, all because she had doted on Chie like a daughter.

"Thank you. Thank you, so much, for—"

"Okay then," she interrupted. "How about we stop procrastinating and get everything going. I need to withdraw the money and get Chie out of here. We may not have that many customers in today, but the cafe needs to be attended to as well."

"Wait, there's just one thing I want to make clear. I'm going to the lookout point, all right? What time did he tell you to be there tonight?" It was the one thing I couldn't cede. I had to go in person, otherwise I wouldn't be able to kill Shiomi. I would take the one million yen for show, but I had no intention of letting him touch it.

"Ten. But he'll be expecting me."

"I'm sure he won't complain, not if I give him the money and don't make a fuss. He needs the money to weasel his way out of whatever situation he's in. I'm going. I just can't let you go, I'm sorry."

She considered this for a while, then nodded. "To be honest, that would be a big relief. I was quite scared."

16

I left the cafe at half past eight. The moon was hidden behind the clouds, but thankfully the rain had stopped. I concentrated on each step, firmly planting my feet as I climbed, using a flashlight to light up the muddy path. The lookout that Shiomi had mentioned was some distance below the peak, at the spot where the meandering mountain road came to an end.

If I followed a narrow path little known to common hikers, it was less than an hour on foot from Shaggy Head to the lookout point. I had wanted more time to plan things carefully, but that couldn't be helped. In my rucksack I had the one million yen from Ms. Hosoya, a long-blade knife I'd taken from the kitchen, a change of clothes, an extra pair of sneakers in case his blood spattered me, a bunch of hand towels from the cafe, and some other small items. I also had my trusty folding mountain knife stuffed in one of the pockets in my chinos.

Ms. Hosoya had gone to the area by the train station to withdraw the money immediately after Shiomi's call. While she was gone I summarized events for Chie and got her ready to leave. She was still a little spaced out, either from the drugs or too much sleep, and helplessly submissive.

I used the outside stairs to sneak out because I knew Na-chi would kick up a fuss if he saw us. I stopped Ms. Hosoya from calling a cab and told her she could use the business car, knowing it would be useful to have for the few days she was looking after Chie. Normally, I tried to keep personal use of the car at a minimum, but the situation had to be taken into account. She seemed a little surprised when I told her it was fine because I was planning to walk to the lookout. Instead of asking why, however, she kept her face solemn and told me to take care.

Naturally, I couldn't drive off in a car emblazoned with Shaggy Head's logo to kill someone. I was proceeding without the necessary preparation, but I still had to be as careful as possible when it came to witnesses, as well as for finger-prints and footprints.

It was far from something I could really call a plan, but I had a rough sketch of what I wanted to do. Ideally I would enter Shiomi's car from the passenger side and stab him while he was still inside the vehicle. In such close quarters I could catch him off guard and thrust the knife in deep, then just drive the corpse away. That was another reason why I had to approach the lookout on foot.

There was also the big issue of what to do with the body once it was done. I had considered various methods I knew from films and books—sinking the car in Osaka Bay, send-ing it off a sharp cliff into a ravine—but in the end decided it would be easiest to make it look like a yakuza hit, taking advantage of Shiomi's current debt issues. That would be easy enough. All I had to do was dump the car and corpse in the city in the sort of place the yakuza used.

Not that everything would necessarily go according to plan. In order to kill him inside the car, I had to first convince him that we needed to exchange the negatives and money in there, but I had no guarantee he would agree to such a thing. The most important thing was to stay flexible, to be able to deal with whatever happened.

I reached the perimeter of the outlook at 9:25, just as I'd planned. I switched the flashlight off and pulled the towel-wrapped knife from my rucksack and slipped it under the back of my belt. I put on a black wool cap, knowing I might get blood in my hair.

A fine, drizzle-like night fog had settled in, dulling the light of the sole streetlamp and the vending machine. On clear nights during this time of year, it was common for couples to arrive in cars and park here in order to enjoy the night cityscape. In tonight's gray fog, however, there was only a single car, parked in the far corner.

Earlier on the phone, Shiomi had told Ms. Hosoya that his car was a silver sedan with a plate that started with the number eight, but from where I was, I couldn't tell if the car I was looking at matched the description. It looked like it might be silver, but maybe it was white. And it was still more than thirty minutes before the agreed time.

I supposed it was a couple looking for some privacy. If it was, I was sure Shiomi would park with enough space between them, so it wouldn't pose an issue for killing him. In fact, having other people nearby would be a good excuse for carrying out the exchange in his car.

I considered all this as I approached the car. I could smell exhaust fumes through the fog, which meant the engine was running. I felt no fear. It surprised me just how composed I was. The sense of tension spreading throughout my body was pleasant, if anything.

I crouched behind the car and switched on my flashlight. Indeed, the body of the car was silver, and the four numbers of the plate started with an eight. I got back to my feet and, keeping a safe distance, circled around to the passenger side.

Something was wrong. I was sure whoever was inside should have noticed me by now, but it didn't feel like anyone was watching me. The engine was still rumbling quietly, but the car was dark inside and I got the sense there was no one inside. The whole vehicle seemed wrong somehow, as though something was deeply and fundamentally out of place. I cautiously edged closer, shining my flashlight in through the glass.

I was right. It was empty.

I wondered if Shiomi had already gotten out, if he was hiding in the woods nearby waiting for the moment to attack. Maybe he had become mad with jealousy from losing Chie to me, and was planning to kill me, just as I was planning to kill him.

As I was thinking this I noticed a blackish stain, something that had at first looked like a shadow in the ring of faint light. There were more stains all over the driver's seat.

I wanted to get a better look. I walked around to the other side, still keeping a cautious stance. I wedged my flashlight under my arm and put on the gloves I had brought with me. I could see through the window that the key was still in the ignition. The doors were unlocked. When I opened a door the

dome lights flicked on and a nauseating stench of blood wafted out.

There was a copious amount. It had spilled down from the
driver's seat to form a deep puddle on the plastic floor mat.
No one could survive such massive blood loss. That was clear
even to me. Someone must have stabbed him multiple times
in the chest and gut while he was still in the driver's seat, exactly as I'd been planning to. The blood spattered on the windows was still fresh and wet. The grisly event had probably
transpired less than an hour ago.

I felt, more than fear, a powerful sense of disappointment.

I was rooted to the spot, half-entertaining the idea that
my alter ego had broken free and killed Shiomi without my
knowledge. Of course, such a thing was impossible. More
than anything, I felt like I had been badly cheated. Not just
cheated—it felt like some con man had tricked me out of a
priceless treasure.

I had no way of releasing all the pent-up energy inside me.
An emotional anchor—my Nan-Core—had been snatched
away from me. What was I supposed to do?

If Shiomi's corpse had been there, I would have pulled
the knife from my belt without hesitation and stabbed him
repeatedly. That was how important it had been to me to kill
him. I needed to bring closure to my feelings towards my
mother, to reinvent myself, to have a future with Chie...

What I ended up doing was to jump into the blood-
soaked car, barely even registering as the soles of my shoes
slid around in the gunk, and to step down on the accelera-
tor. I frantically spun the steering wheel around, barely able
to contain my heart as it pounded hard enough to burst, and

drove the car down the winding mountain road, going as fast as I possibly could. I was continuing with the rest of my plan, moving on to the next stage as though I had killed Shiomi myself.

It was the only choice I had.

I realized it was the yakuza. They'd beaten me to the very crime I was going to frame them with. Yet it was impossible to do nothing, to just leave the car and stroll nonchalantly back down the mountain.

It took twenty minutes to reach the bottom of the mountain road, and I didn't pass a single car during that time. Halfway down, the choking stench became unbearable, and I rolled down all the windows a third of the way. The driver's seat had sucked up the blood like a sea sponge, and as I sat there the blood soaked into my clothes until they clung to my back and rear. My white gloves were stained dark.

I used backstreets wherever possible, taking local roads for a while before switching onto the expressway for Osaka. Feeling the blood as it wet my skin, breathing in the smell of it, I began to feel intoxicated by a sense of victory. Inside the car with all that blood, it wasn't hard to persuade myself that I'd been the one to kill Shiomi. I could somehow vividly sense in my hand the lingering feeling of the knife plunging deep between his ribs.

"Yes! Yes! Yesss!" I shouted with exhilaration at myself, banging the steering wheel with my gloved hands.

I exited the expressway at Minatomachi, knowing the area was surprisingly quiet once you moved away from the Namba JR train station. Low office buildings around four or five stories tall were crammed alongside the tracks, and at this time of night the place would be devoid of people or traffic.

As I drove around in search of a place to dump the car, the fluorescent lights atop the telephone poles here and there made the streets look like a scene from a black-and-white movie. I felt a chill when I passed a vending machine, the only source of color, and a police car appeared from the right-hand side of a narrow intersection. Although we were nowhere near a collision we both hit our brakes, and then I crossed the intersection first, as the left side has priority. I kept my eyes ahead and drove slowly, but I was afraid they might think it suspicious that I was wearing a woolen cap when it wasn't winter.

After I'd driven for a while I broke out in a cold sweat. If they'd stopped me for questioning, that would have been game over. That area had occasional violent crimes that got covered in the papers, so it was only natural that the police had a robust presence. I couldn't keep roaming the area in case I came across the same cruiser again. I drove back to the tracks to get a better sense of the area, still heading away from the station. Then I crossed the tracks at a random junction and looped back towards the station.

A large, fenced-off plot of land appeared ahead on the left, and I pulled in without a moment's thought. Luck was with me as the entrance wasn't gated. I drove around the plot in a slow circle, using my headlights to illuminate the area.

The grass had been left to run wild but the land wasn't completely vacant. It looked like a construction site abandoned in the middle of laying the foundation. There were a number of concrete pipes and other miscellaneous building materials left exposed to the elements and even a pre-fab construction shed. I'd expected to find places like this in an area undergoing redevelopment, where construction on a project had been cancelled partway through when its prospects had dimmed. I would have probably found one straightaway, but at night it was harder to see long distances.

For some strange reason there was a fridge, an electric kettle, and some plastic storage bins jumbled in among a heap of abandoned construction materials off to one side. Next to that was a couple of vehicles parked nose to nose, one a station wagon, the other a sedan, both slightly blackened. They were half-buried with weeds up to the windows, so I supposed they had been abandoned as well.

It was exactly what I needed.

I picked out a suitable area and drove slowly into the undergrowth, letting the bumper plow through the grass. I rolled up the windows, turned off the engine, and got out of the car. I pulled my rucksack from the backseat and locked the doors.

Outside, I took a few deep breaths of the grass-scented air.

The blood was drying out like glue, making my clothes stick to me. It mingled with my sweat, creating a terrible smell. I wondered what kind of face Yohei would make if he saw me like this. My mouth twisted into a laughing sob as the thought came to me.

I stripped off my cap, shirt, pants, underwear, and shoes, then used all twenty of the plastic-wrapped wipes I'd brought from the cafe to scrub my body down, starting with my hands and face. I needed many more wipes, but it couldn't be helped.

Anything with blood on it got bundled into a plastic garbage bag, ready to burn in the incinerator at the cafe. Once I was wearing the fresh change of clothes and a clean pair of sneakers, I started to feel a little better.

I had to call Ms. Hosoya since she would be waiting for me to report in. It was already well past eleven. I wasn't too far from the train tracks, so I was afraid she might notice the sound if a train passed by. I called regardless.

"Oh, you're okay! What on earth took you so long?" I'd never heard her sound so harsh.

"Sorry to call so late. Shiomi didn't show. I waited all this time for nothing. I've been on edge the whole time, so I'm totally exhausted." I didn't have the energy to hate myself for lying. I was working under the illusion, even then, that I had killed Shiomi. I was still carrying out my plan as though that had been the case.

"Oh, he didn't? What happened? He'd sounded so desperate for the money."

"Don't know. Maybe he found another way."

Ms. Hosoya seemed to consider this, and when she spoke again her tone was more relaxed. "Well, anyways, we kept our side of the bargain. I don't think there's anything more to do at this point. We'll just have to wait. No doubt he'll be back with more threats very soon."

If day after day came and went with no further contact from Shiomi, would Ms. Hosoya and Chie regain their peace of mind and gradually forget about him? As I considered this, a doubt crossed my mind for the first time—was that blood really Shiomi's? I turned back without thinking, the phone still pressed to my ear, and regarded the car I'd left in the middle of the flattened weeds. I hadn't stabbed him, so I couldn't be sure. There was a greater-than-zero possibility, in theory, that Shiomi had killed the yakuza who'd been following him. He might have used the other car to escape. I pondered this with a mind that felt like it was waking from a dream. If that was true, I would have inadvertently helped Shiomi cover up his own crime.

I felt on the verge of panic just for a moment, but managing to keep my voice calm I asked, "How is Chie doing?"

"Sleeping now, thanks to the pills. She ate all of her dinner, too. She should start getting better soon, physically at least."

I asked if she was still happy to look after Chie for a few more days as we'd originally agreed. If we didn't hear from Shiomi during that time, it was probably safe to assume he was dead. The negatives I'd failed to retrieve weighed heavily on my mind, but I couldn't do anything about that for now.

"Are you still at the lookout?" she asked, just as I was about to hang up.

"Yes. I'm going to head back down now."

"Be careful. And there's no point in thinking about things too much. Have a bath or something, get some proper rest tonight."

"I just might. Thank you."

I checked the time again: just before midnight. It would be cutting it close, but if I sprinted I could just make the last train out of Namba.

17

Everything was suddenly peaceful again. Five days passed, then ten, and as I'd expected there was no word from Shiomi.

The weather was hot and clear. For a few hours during midday the dog run was empty, but it was almost overfull in the mornings and evenings. With kids on summer vacation coming in as well, Shaggy Head was busier than at any other time of the year.

I read the papers carefully but had yet to find any articles on a suspicious, blood-soaked car being discovered around Namba. If, unluckily enough, someone noticed the car and reported it to the police, they would soon find out it belonged to Shiomi, and as Chie was his wife according to his family register, it was possible a detective would show up to ask questions. Or they might come to question me, since I was the one she was having an affair with.

None of this worried me. They could look anywhere, do whatever they liked—I was sure they wouldn't find a single clue. That would be true even in the rare case that someone found his corpse floating in Osaka Bay. No evidence existed that could link us to the murder.

As for the car, I felt sure it would just stay there unnoticed for a long time yet, as the grass gradually buried it. I imagined the blood of the man who had ruined Chie's life roasting under a blazing sun, drying up, then starting to crack like blackened coal tar.

I felt a bizarre sense of accomplishment, as if I'd actually pulled off what I'd set out to do. I understood that I hadn't killed Shiomi. Even though I hadn't actually carried out the act, I couldn't shake the feeling that by sheer force of will my desire to kill him had brought about the result. It wasn't logical, I just wanted to believe it was true. I had to believe it. Who cared if it was a delusion? The physiological sensations were still there, branded into me: the smell of the blood, the tackiness as it stuck to my skin.

Ms. Hosoya only took three days off work but out of an abundance of caution let Chie stay for a week, until the cafe closed for the *O-bon* holiday. On the last night we had what felt like a celebratory dinner at her place.

I was stuffing my cheeks with Chie's home-cooked pizza when I told them I suspected Shiomi had been killed by the yakuza, and that was why we hadn't heard from him. Chie, who still hadn't fully recovered from her absentminded state, put her raised glass back on the table and frowned a little.

Ms. Hosoya looked at us both in turn before letting out a sigh. "You're probably right. He was scared out of his wits. Maybe he didn't have the time to come and get the money. A pitiful end to a pitiful man."

That was the last time the three of us ever spoke of Shiomi.

The bruises on Chie's ribs, shoulders, and thighs yellowed

and started to fade, but it looked like it would be a long while before they vanished altogether. She began to apply a light amount of makeup again like before. We were in the kitchen nearly daily during the five-day holiday, preparing lots of food from time-consuming recipes. We gave the kitchen a thorough cleaning, even the corners we didn't usually get to, and painstakingly polished the glass in all the cafe's windows and doors.

At least for the holidays, I wanted to forget about stuff like cleaning Shaggy Head's windows, not to mention all the cooking, but Chie seemed the most at ease when we kept ourselves occupied like that. When we did relax and listen to music, Chie usually fell asleep. Once asleep she would doze for a couple of hours, then sleep the whole night without taking any pills. It seemed to me that the more she slept, the more the color returned to her eyes, and the more her face looked tranquil.

We still didn't say much to each other, except for discussing the steps needed for cooking or cleaning. We relied on simple gestures and looks to communicate the many things we couldn't express in words, and for the most part it worked fine. I supposed we might talk someday, little by little, about the time we were apart, what had happened, what we had thought then. That clearly wouldn't happen for a while. But when that time came I wanted Chie to know all about my mother and the notebooks she had left.

I doubted, however, that I would tell her about that night, about the blood-soaked midnight drive. It was my secret, something neither Chie nor Ms. Hosoya could ever know.

The last night of the holidays, Chie and I made love for

the first time since we'd been reunited. We were both nervous, awkward. For Chie it seemed to be a necessary formality, something to help her begin to move on.

"I'm sorry," she said in a faint voice, and started to tremble. "Don't you hate this? You know that I…"

I didn't want to force her into anything and break the gentle equilibrium that still held between us. And yet I wanted her so badly it felt like I might burst into flames. Hardly able to control myself, I was at a loss for what to do. I held her closer, ignoring my urges as I stroked her back for a long time. I kept whispering "It's gonna be all right" into her ear until her trembling subsided.

It's gonna be all right.

They were the words Dad had whispered to my mother the first night they made love. I had known that and said them anyway, because there was no better phrase to use at such a moment.

The night is young, there's no need to rush. It's gonna be all right. I repeated it for my own benefit, like an incantation. I brought my lips to Chie's, which were wet with tears.

One day when it was raining for the first time in a while and business was slow, I called Yohei.

"Hey, Ryo. You never got back to me. I was wondering what happened to you." He sounded grumpy. It was before noon so he'd probably been asleep.

"You could have called me if you were worried."

"Nah, not worth the effort."

As blunt as ever.

Yohei and I were cousins, I supposed, not even brothers.

I knew I would never be able to change the brotherly feelings I felt for him. I wondered how it would be for him. For that matter, had he figured out the truth yet?

"I went to see Dad the day before last. I thought about asking you along, but..."

"Why didn't you? How was he?"

"Really, really thin. I kind of..."

"Oh," I muttered in response, but my words trailed off, too. I remembered the last time I'd seen him, how deathly pale his face had looked.

"I... I went with Miyuki. Wanted him to see her, while he's still well enough," he said unexpectedly, sounding despondent.

"Miyuki? The one you called Myukki, who dumped you ages ago?"

"Of course. Obviously."

"Okay."

"We bumped into each other on the bullet train when I went to pick up the family register."

"Really?"

"She was on her way to visit some relatives in Nagoya, but she changed her mind and came with me instead. She said she'd never been on the Hato Tour Bus, ever."

"The Hato Tour Bus?" I was dumbstruck, nearly literally. So that was why Yohei had suddenly wanted to stay overnight in Tokyo. "And had you ever taken it yourself?"

"Nope."

Yohei had dated Miyuki for a while right after the start of freshman year of college. She was two years his senior at the same school. He'd been a surprisingly late bloomer and she was his first girlfriend. After about a year they suddenly stopped seeing each other—I don't know what happened—and she graduated not long afterwards.

"And what you just said about her dumping me? It was the other way around. I dumped her. How many times have I told you that?"

"Oh, is that so? Even though you dumped her, you spent a hell of a long time down in the dumps, and even had to repeat a year. And you kept howling her name when you drank—'Myukki, Myukki!'"

"I already told you, that was because I realized she'd forced me to dump her."

"Yeah, and normally that's referred to as 'getting dumped.'"

"And I've stopped calling her Myukki. So don't call her that."

"Oh, really. Why's that?"

"You'll find out when you see her. It doesn't really suit her anymore. Nope, not at all."

Myukki was a cutesy name, and, as far as I knew, Miyuki didn't quite have the looks to pull it off. She was short and rather unattractive, to be honest. When I first met her I couldn't work out why Yohei had chosen her as his first girlfriend, but the confusion soon gave way to understanding after we'd chatted a while. It wasn't just that she was smart, she had her own unique energy, a sensitivity that was quicksilver, like shoals of fish darting through her head.

"That's all good, just don't run away this time."

"Yeah."

I'd expected him to talk back; the one-word response

left me feeling startled. I supposed he wouldn't care about the notebooks or the stuff in the family register now, not if he was in love again. I was sure he would notice things eventually, but that was that, and I decided to leave it alone for now.

"I've got some news, too. Chie came back."

"No way."

"Yes, way. She's been through a lot. I'll tell you all about it sometime."

After the *O-bon* holiday, Chie had recommenced her work at the cafe. Nachi and the other part-timers took her reappearance in stride. I only had to rush in and intervene once; Nachi, spouting some nonsense about how an old flame being rekindled makes for an even sturdier foundation, had proceeded to try to hug her. The dogs remembered her, too— they tried to outdo one another in expressing how glad they were to see her, trying to lick her hands and enthusiastically wagging their tails.

"Wow, that's great news, Ryo. Really great news." It sounded like he was exaggerating a bit, but I didn't mind. "I was really worried, you know. I thought it would be cruel to tell you about Miyuki. You weren't yourself after Chie ran away, I didn't want to add to that."

"But you just told me."

"Yeah, well, I thought you might try to steal Miyuki away from me if you saw how she is now."

"Like I would, you moron."

"You can't say that until you've seen her. Never can be too careful around love-starved men."

"This from the guy who was always giving Chie lustful looks."

"That wasn't lust, just affection for my future sister-in-law."

"Sure, sure," I said, about to take the opportunity to end the call when Yohei suggested the four of us all go for dinner soon.

Then he added, almost as an afterthought, "Oh and I don't care if you're my brother, cousin, or just some random stranger. You never were the typical elder-brother type, so I guess I've always considered you a life-long best friend."

So he was just as shrewd as I'd hoped. He'd figured it out. I could almost see his smug look on the other end of the line, feeling he'd got one up on me. Despite his not knowing how the author of those notebooks had died.

"Life-long best friends? That's not bad. It makes me happy to hear you say it. So I guess we're splitting the bill from now on when we go out for steak?"

I heard him swallow, but he didn't respond.

"So, I'm looking forward to seeing Myu—sorry, Miyuki. Let me know when you've settled on a date. I'm always free in the evenings."

I hung up, holding back a laugh. I paused for a breath, then brought the phone back up to my ear.

"Hey, so it's you." Dad's deep, gravelly voice was the same as when he'd been well.

"I won't ask how you're doing."

"That's appreciated, thanks."

"I hear Yohei came over with a girl."

"Yeah, Miyuki, she came over several times way back when. You met her, right? Full of life, she is. Talking to her makes me feel spry myself."

Our conversation lingered on Yohei for a while, about how the girls he'd become involved with after his split with Miyuki had all been good-looking, like models, but had never lasted beyond a few months. Yohei always said they were the ones leaving him, but I suspected he was the one doing the running away. I thought he was afraid of the relationships getting serious.

"Well. I never knew he went through so many girlfriends."

"In the end, it was only Miyuki he ever brought to see you."

"So maybe this time, just maybe, this is it."

"Listen, Dad. Chie came back." I'd been trying to work out a good time to bring it up, but in the end I just blurted it out.

"I see." That was all he said. He didn't ask anything else. His reaction made it sound like he already knew.

"I'll bring her over soon."

"I always knew she would, you know. I knew she'd come back to you eventually. I'm glad she made it in time."

I had to admit Miyuki had indeed changed, although she still wasn't so awe-inspiring she shouldn't be called "Myukki." I think she had probably realized how fruitless it was to try and play up her feminine side. She'd cut off all her long, permed curls and wore her hair short, her face was free of makeup, and she wore a tank top that clearly showed off her flat chest. It was like she was laughing out loud, making an open declaration of who she was. I still couldn't say she was beautiful, but she was striking in a way that would have been impossible if she had been beautiful.

She's definitely something.

Right?

Yohei and I exchanged looks, speaking with our eyes as we chewed our steaks.

I guessed she was a lot more comfortable in her own skin now. Her keen, logical wit was the same, not even a step behind Yohei's, but her former tendency to take pleasure in arguing people down had abated, and she enjoyed herself more freely as she joked and verbally sparred with everyone else.

It was great when the four of us got together to eat, drink, and have fun. Chie and Miyuki got on immediately, and after a while, they started to hang out together to watch tearjerker movies or shop flea markets and to do other things Yohei and I weren't interested in.

They both liked to cook, and one time they prepared a bunch of different dishes that we brought with us on a visit to Dad. We laid the table and drank some beer, and the drab house echoed with laughter. Dad looked like he was really enjoying himself. We didn't stay for very long. By the time he saw us off at the door, it was plainly evident to everyone that he was completely exhausted.

On the way to the station I told Yohei, "That was probably the last time we could do something like that."

After that I dropped in to see him every now and again. Much of the time I bumped into Yohei who was doing the same. Although Dad was taking the medicine the hospital had prescribed, he continued to refuse to be admitted. He wouldn't try any new drugs or alternative treatments or go to another hospital for a second opinion. We both stopped trying to force him into things.

When the three of us were in the kitchen, drinking beer and chatting about nothing in particular, it felt very familial. We shared a comfortableness with one another that seemed to soften the edges of our emotions.

The photograph of Mom watched us from its place on the small bureau in the living room. Whenever my eyes drifted that way during a lull in the conversation, my heart filled with warm nostalgia. In reality she was my aunt, Emiko. But just as Yohei was still my kid brother, I knew she would remain as my other mother for the rest of my life. I could never forget all the years we spent together, all the years she spent loving me unconditionally. I didn't know what mad thoughts had been swirling through her head that time she watched me sleep with the pillow clutched to her chest. Even if her thoughts had turned to murder, I was no longer naive enough to think that that negated her love for me.

So much had happened in so little time. It felt as though I had aged ten, maybe even twenty years all at once.

A murderous prostitute, a passerby client. I asked myself what I felt for these people, my real parents, but I never came up with a viable answer. All I felt was a knotted mess of contradictory emotions. I supposed the answer would never be clear for the rest of my life.

Some part of me wondered if getting old meant embracing chaos for what it was, bringing it close and living with it. Maybe part of maturing was learning that the human heart is forever unfathomable and itself a form of chaos.

The summer passed slowly.

The cafe grew busier, new members joining practically by

the week. Ms. Hosoya said that Chie's return broke whatever jinx it was that had cast its shadow on Shaggy Head.

"We couldn't expect business to thrive with our key member, the boss, looking as down as you did. Everything's all better now," Ms. Hosoya said, and she herself seemed more cheerful. She would often give a faint smile as she watched Chie running busily between the tables.

One night, when Chie and I were relaxing in my room, I said, "This is just a suspicion I have, but I sometimes wonder if Ms. Hosoya lost a daughter or something."

"Why?"

"She just dotes on you so much, and it makes me think: Did she experience something like that in her past? Like, I wonder if she had a daughter who would be your age if she were still alive."

Maybe losing her daughter had been one of the reasons behind her divorce. Or maybe she hadn't been able to get pregnant even though she'd really wanted a baby girl.

I was running such groundless ideas through my head when Chie quietly said, "She's really kind, isn't she." Her voice was filled with emotion. "I'm so grateful for everything she did that it's hard to put into words."

"I feel the same."

"I didn't know you thought about it like that, though. That she saw me as a lost daughter."

"It's pure conjecture. What about you? Do you ever feel anything like that from her?"

"I think you're right, that she thinks of me as a daughter. But probably not in the way you think."

"How so?"

Chie angled her head as she looked at me, then chuckled. "You're surprisingly slow sometimes, Ryosuke."

"Where the hell did that come from?"

"Ms. Hosoya likes you. She's in love with you."

"Hey, wait... What?"

"There's the age difference, of course, and she knows she can't let you find out. She's the type who can make rational decisions like that. But I knew immediately how she felt about you."

"But... But that's totally... Come on, if that was the case, how could she be so nice to you? She'd be jealous."

"I suppose, but that's why she's so amazing. She's self-aware enough to know she can't be with you, so I think she's entrusted her dream to me. She thinks of me as a daughter, a kind of extension of herself. By making sure you and I stay together she's seeking her own fulfillment. That way, instead of being jealous, she can do her best to make us both happy."

I didn't want to believe what she was saying.

"Maybe people can do such things when they truly love someone. You'd probably have chosen her over me if she was younger."

"Impossible. You're the only one for me."

"But you really didn't notice? Not even a glimpse of something in the way she acts around you?"

That made me remember the time I helped Ms. Hosoya up after she'd been knocked down by Cujo, the large Bernese. I had held her slender body in my arms and noticed that some of the buttons on her blouse had come undone, giving me a view of the pale-white skin of her chest. I would be lying if I said I didn't feel anything in that moment. And when she wrapped her arms around my neck, didn't I feel a sudden dizzying sense of depth, like I was being pulled into something? Nachi, too, believed that Ms. Hosoya kissed me on purpose…

"Oh, Ryosuke, you've gone red!" Chie said, sounding a little surprised.

18

Now and then I was racked with anxiety about the negatives I'd failed to retrieve from Shiomi. I was scared that some heartless bastard might spread the compromising pictures of Chie around the internet. I was sure Ms. Hosoya shared the same fears, but we never discussed the matter. After what Chie had said I lost the ability to act normally around her. Whenever we ended up alone together, I pretended to suddenly remember something and fled, even though I knew I was being stupid about it. I don't know if she noticed my odd behavior; she continued to work diligently and seemed perfectly at ease.

After the autumn equinox we still had a few days that were as hot as summer. That didn't stop the dogs from running around the field and gulping down water from the faucet. Their animal instincts apparently judged mid-80's weather to be cooler in autumn than during the summer.

The seasons changing day by day felt relentlessly cruel. I supposed this was due to having an illness in the family. I couldn't prevent the sick from getting worse any more than I could halt the progress of autumn. Each time I thought this might be the last time Dad saw the fall foliage, I couldn't stop myself from getting upset.

It was relatively easier to take time off work now that Chie was back at Shaggy Head. I wanted to see Dad every day if possible, but he was becoming more and more stubborn as his condition worsened, and he got ornery if we visited too often. He would tell us not to treat him like an invalid, even though he had weakened to the point where he could hardly open a jar of jam.

It didn't take Yohei much effort to loosen the lid, but when he did he lost control, bursting into tears. Before our visit Dad had spent three days eating plain toast for breakfast, having taken a sudden dislike to the smell of butter and wanting jam instead.

"Don't cry." Yohei's head was on the table and Dad gave him a gentle smile as he stroked it, making a mess of his cat-like hair. "I can feel that I'm falling apart, but nothing hurts. It's funny. Sometimes I wonder if I'm not getting off too easily. So there's no need to worry. No need to get worked up over me."

He was silent for a while as he ran his fingers through Yohei's hair, pinching clumps of it into spikes. He ruffled it back to normal, then said to me, "If you can come all this way you should go see your grandmother, too. I won't be able to visit her for much longer. I know I don't have much to leave you, and I'm sorry to push the responsibility onto you, but look after her, okay?"

I couldn't imagine how the end might come for Dad. If he continued to refuse to be hospitalized, he would probably spend his last moments in the house. Would we know, the closer it got, when it was likely to happen? Or would it be sudden, leaving us filled with regret for not having had the chance to say goodbye? All that was left to wish for was that he wouldn't be by himself, feeling lonely, when it happened.

That day on the way home I asked Yohei to dinner. Even after a steak, however, he failed to return to his usual cheery self. We talked in clipped sentences about the reality we had to face. Once that was done I told him everything Dad had said about Misako, my mother. I was the one who told him about the notebooks when he'd known nothing about them, even forcing him to read sections. It was unfair to involve him as far as I had and not tell him how it ended.

He already knew enough to work out we were in fact cousins. I couldn't leave him feeling unsettled about everything, not when we were preparing to say goodbye to Dad.

"You're not surprised?" I asked once I'd finished, noting that his expression was unchanged.

"Of course I am. I had wondered as much. But still, it's hard to believe."

"What do you think about it?"

"That there was no hate. That it's a chronicle of family love." I wasn't sure what he meant, but I stopped myself from asking again.

He was right, I supposed, that no one had hated anyone else. Even though the others had killed my mother, they had done it so she could atone for her sins while simultaneously offering her salvation. Perhaps that was what he meant.

"I'm glad you told me, Ryo."

I nodded, feeling very relieved somehow.

Following Dad's wishes that we focus on visiting Gran, Yohei and I made an effort to see her more often. She no longer seemed able to tell us apart—she didn't even seem to understand that we were her grandchildren. At the same time, she seemed happy to have young people coming in to fuss over her. Now and again she opened her toothless mouth to offer us an innocent, child-like smile. We were keen to help, even when it was just with food, in contrast to having unwittingly assigned the various chores to Dad.

After a process of trial and error we discovered we worked best together, Yohei using the spoon to feed her, I wiping any mess off her chin from the side. When we established a rhythm, Gran managed to get through her entire dinner without leaving a thing. One time, when a staff member came to check in on us, Yohei even complained about the spoons. He said the home needed to provide spoons of different shapes and sizes depending on the type of food served. The staffer walked out after mumbling a noncommittal response.

Whenever the home had a singer volunteering or a women's chorus performing in the auditorium, we bundled Gran into a wheelchair and took her to watch. Some of the others gathered there would quietly sing along, nostalgic for the old songs, some clapping in time. Gran's head, looking like she was wearing a white woolly cap, would sway above her chair as well.

Everything that had befallen her family was engraved inside that small head, all the memories from Misako's birth up to her death. Now her mind was a disembodied shadow wandering through an amorphous fog.

Sometimes, though, when she suddenly gazed off into empty space with a frightened look or burst into tears without warning, I had to wonder whether the thorns of those memories were still lodged inside her head, scratching and painful in her shattered consciousness.

19

I had a rare call from Dad one morning when the days were starting to get bitterly cold both in the mornings and at night.

"I said my goodbyes to Gran yesterday. I told her I wouldn't be able to visit anymore."

"Oh." I wanted to say something kind that would express how I felt, but I knew he'd hate that.

"I'm terribly weak now. I want to see you both, one last time. There are some things I want to tell you."

"Okay."

"The forecast says it's going to rain this afternoon. I'm sure it'll be slow at the cafe, so could you come over?"

"Yeah, sure."

"Did you have a talk with Yohei?"

"I told him everything about what was in the notebooks and what you told me."

"When was this?"

"Quite a while back now. Probably a couple of months. He's smart, so I think he'd already had a pretty good idea. Didn't seem all that surprised."

"I see. He's amazing, you know, he hasn't breathed a word about it to me. Still, it's for the best. Gran won't be around for much longer, you'll be the only blood relations left. It's better for you both to know everything going forward."

"You don't have to worry, we'll be okay."

"I'm not worried. Invite him along, will you? Come over after lunch. I'll be waiting here."

This is an odd thing to say, but as his condition deteriorated, what made Dad "Dad" seemed to grow more concentrated, becoming more apparent in his various expressions. The obstinacy, the child-like qualities, the mad-scientist-like way he was sometimes out of touch with reality, and his unique gentleness.

He was terribly skinny but still had a kind of dignity. As always, I couldn't tell what he was thinking, but I knew he wasn't afraid of dying. Yohei and I were nervous, aware he had hinted at seeing us for the last time. We sat around the table in the kitchen but hardly touched the snacks of fish paste and salami on the plates and didn't refill our beer glasses. Dad was the only one who seemed livelier than usual.

"Misako came to visit."

He said this like it was something to be expected.

He'd said "Misako," but I didn't know which of my two mothers he meant. I wondered if he'd started to lose his mind, either from the illness or the pills he was taking. Yohei was gaping at him.

Dad paid us no mind. He began to talk, pausing only to catch his breath as he told us an incredible story.

A while ago I told Ryosuke about what happened to Misako.

There is actually a lot more to tell. I couldn't decide whether to tell you the rest. To be honest I'm still not sure if I should. Maybe if you'd been totally ignorant from the start, it'd be different, but now that you know some of what happened, I think it would be insolent to cover up the rest of it.

First and foremost, I don't want to have to think this over anymore, not when I'm facing death. Ryosuke, and Yohei, I want you to consider this my last will and testament as you listen.

As I just said, Misako came to visit yesterday. Yes, your birth mother, Ryosuke. Yes, the woman who wrote the notebooks. We've been seeing each other every now and then for a few years. I'm not going to make excuses. I just…had to. Knowing I don't have much time left, she asked me to go on a trip, to make one last memory together. It's exactly what I want, but I asked her to wait until tomorrow. I wanted the time to talk to you first.

Now, hang on—this won't make sense unless I tell you everything in order. If I know her, she'll be back later. If you want you can meet her, but you don't have to. Maybe you'll be okay, Yohei, but I imagine Ryosuke might need more than a day to prepare himself.

There's just one more thing to say first: I gave the notebooks, the hair, and the handbag to Misako and asked her to get rid of them. Okay? They shouldn't be left around. I wanted to burn it all myself, but this house doesn't have anywhere to build a proper fire.

It happened a long while ago. Misako just appeared out of nowhere. I was on my way back from work, about to head through the turnstiles, when she called my name. It had been ten years, and I'd thought her dead the whole time. I stood in the middle of the crowd and reached out to touch her cheek, to assure myself she wasn't an illusion. The moment I made contact it was like those ten years just up and vanished.

I knew immediately that times had been hard for her. Her expression had changed completely. Where her features had been ill-defined before there was a severe virility. I suppose it's odd to describe a woman's face as looking virile. She didn't laugh much, just like before, but when she did it was from the heart. I'd never seen her do that.

We talked, wandering through the streets near the station. I asked straightaway how she'd found me. She told me she knew we were in Komagawa. She'd guessed I would take the train from Komagawa or transfer on my way to work, and she'd been looking for me there that morning. When she actually spotted me she considered going home, but she ended up following after me to see where I got off. She spent the rest of the day walking around, hesitant and unsure of what to do, but she went back to the station in the evening. That's apparently what happened.

I asked where she was living and how she knew we were living in Komagawa, but instead of answering she made it clear she was very keen to hear about the family. I mainly talked about you, Ryosuke. You were still in middle school then. Then I told her you had a younger brother, Yohei, about Emiko, and about her parents, who were both alive and well. I became so engrossed in telling her these things that time flew by.

Looking back now, that was so strange. I'd conspired with her family to kill her, yet there we were. Plus her younger sister Emiko had assumed her identity, and she had had our son, Yohei. Despite all that there wasn't even a trace of awkwardness between us.

Misako listened with rapt attention, smiling with tears in her eyes. She was completely immersed in my stories. I just kept talking, knowing she was very interested in what I was saying.

When I finally reached a convenient point to pause, I asked

what had happened to her—in other words, after her parents had driven her away in the car. She seemed surprised to find out that I knew nothing about it, but she told me anyway. It was an amazing story, and she told it matter-of-factly, as though it was a simple catch-up on how she was doing.

She said she thought she'd been sucked into the well. You know, the old well she wrote about in the notebooks, in the garden of the house of the girl who died, Michiru. As she sank to the bottom of the lake behind the dam, her hands and legs tied up, she thought that the dark well of death had finally caught up to her, that it would pull her down forever. Your grandparents had given her a large dose of sleeping pills to ease any suffering. Her mind was probably groggy from that.

She told me it was terrifying. She lost all sensation until nothing she could call her self remained. That was when she died. She knew it for certain, she said.

She was lying on her side when she came to in a totally unfamiliar place. She wondered if it was already night as everything around her was pitch dark. Her heart felt empty. She was still tied up so she couldn't move.

Then she heard a voice.

"Don't turn around. Just keep quiet and listen."

It was a hoarse male voice, and for some reason she thought it was me: I'd jumped into the well; my voice was like that because I'd had a hard time getting her out.

It wasn't me, regrettably. I never asked him directly, but I think it was probably your grandfather. I can't see it being anyone else. Your grandmother would have known, of course. After throwing her into the water, they must have found they couldn't just leave their daughter to die.

"You're a criminal, having you around creates disaster for everyone. If you care for your son's future, never have anything to do with your family ever again. As of today, you must become another person and live another life. Concentrate on nothing but atoning for your sins," the voice continued.

The words settled in her empty, newly-revived heart.

The man behind the voice loosened the ropes around her arms and legs before leaving. She waited a while, then shuffled free, got to her feet, and started to walk. Her shoes had been neatly arranged by her side.

Her legs were trembling so badly that she had to rest every few steps. She noticed she was freezing because her clothes were still wet. She found a bundle of ten-thousand-yen notes in one of her soaked pockets, as well as a hastily scribbled map on a scrap of paper that outlined the way back to the city.

Her strength gave out partway through her journey, and she slept that night in some bushes next to the road. When she finally reached the city the next day she boarded a train, hoping to get as far away as she could. With no particular destination in mind she changed trains a number of times, finally getting off at a deserted station, the name of which she'd never heard of. It was already evening.

She called home using a pay phone at the station. The man behind the voice—she still thought it was me—had forbidden her from doing so, but she was desperate to know how you, Ryosuke, were doing since your transfer to the hospital in Tokyo. She needed to hear it before she could move on to become someone else. They hadn't let her see you properly since the night of the incident.

Gran answered the phone. She was breathing heavily when she said Misako's name, sounding like she had to force it out. Then she immediately composed herself, rapidly answering Misako's questions.

"You don't need to worry about Ryosuke... He'll be in the hospital for a while but it's nothing serious... He's doing well." Her voice grew muffled with tears partway through but she kept to a whisper, apparently fearing your grandfather might overhear.

That was when Gran told her about Komagawa. "Your father will be furious if he ever finds out I let you know," she warned her before telling her the place. She explained that Emiko and I were going to move there soon, and that we'd look after you, Ryosuke, there. "So there's no need to worry, I want you to live your life. If you care about Ryosuke's happiness, then stay away. Never break that rule, no matter what happens. But I'll still pray that someday something will bring us back together again, even if just for a moment. I'll always pray for that," she said through tears.

It's all a bit incoherent, I know. But she was still Misako's mother, even after everything that happened. She would have felt pity for her daughter, who was being forced to live as a wretched recluse.

She can't tell Emiko and Misako apart anymore, not with the dementia, but she does seem to remember, if only vaguely, the fact that she did something awful to one of her own daughters. She's still suffering from that, even now. I can tell.

Sorry, that's a bit off topic. So, after the call, Misako obeyed what the male voice had said. She had worked out on her own that Emiko would need to take her place as your mother and my wife, understanding it was necessary for the family—all five of us—to start over in a new land. She also believed it was the best for you, Ryosuke.

She understood that she shouldn't have been allowed to live, so it didn't matter. She wasn't even human, just a corpse that had been revived by some chance. She carved that concept into her mind.

"You're a criminal, having you around creates disaster for everyone." Misako repeated the words the man had spoken over and over to herself.

I don't have the time or strength to go through all the details of her life after that. She spent a while drifting from place to place, then worked for a long time as a live-in maid at a hot springs resort town in the Tohoku region. She was greatly helped, she said, by the kindness of others.

Without a resident card or a family register she was unable to get a license or certifications necessary for gainful employment. There's no way she didn't lead a hard life. And yet she told me that the things that once scared her didn't anymore, now that she'd escaped unscathed from the dark well. Hard work didn't feel difficult because she was a corpse, and as for her Nan-Core, she was now perfectly fine without one. It was uncanny. The woman before me was Misako, yet not Misako. The woman I met was another Misako.

You can probably imagine what happened. It wasn't fair to your late mother, but I had never—not for a moment—forgotten about Misako. Your mother realized this, of course, and I know she suffered as a result. But I couldn't do anything about it. I don't know, people can be really horrid.

I think Misako had been the same. She had been acting tough for so long that hardship no longer felt like hardship, but there must have been something deep in her heart that she couldn't erase. She lived like an actual zombie for three, five, then ten years, but that something continued to grow until the day came that she couldn't suppress it any longer. Why else would she have turned up out of nowhere like that?

She had told herself it would be the one and only time she'd see me or ask after you. And I could tell she knew perfectly well it was unforgivable in itself.

We'd been walking non-stop for two hours and found ourselves back in front of the train station. She said goodbye and bowed, and just like that she turned to leave. She'd taken maybe a dozen steps when I realized what was happening and called out to stop her. I called her name, loudly enough to make a few passersby turn.

"I want to see you again, even if it's just once a year. I'll bring photos of Ryosuke and the family and update you on how we're doing," I said.

She laughed and said it would be like *Tanabata*, the annual summer festival of star-crossed lovers, and suggested we take it a step further and meet at the same station at 5 p.m. every July 7th. Once a year, for just a few hours. We would share the burden of her sins.

She told me she didn't want me to ask anything about her current life when we met, and I agreed.

It was October then, so it was less than a year until the next *Tanabata*. That made it bearable. It was hard to wait. At the same time I was euphoric, elated to have discovered that this woman I had thought dead was still alive. We were apart, but we were still under the same sky. You both know I'm not religious, but I still felt gratitude to a higher something for the way things had turned out.

Each year I brought family photos as promised. I spent my days thinking up all sorts of things to say when we met, only to forget it all when the time came. We only ever discussed mundane things. Even though we didn't have much time, we sat next to each other and watched the city lights in silence for long spells. I kept my word, never once asking where she was living or what she was doing. She didn't have the luxury of being picky about what jobs she took, and it was evident that her life was hard. If I'd known any of it, I wouldn't have been able to stop myself from trying to help. I wanted to avoid that. We both knew it was betrayal enough just to be meeting.

I don't want you two to get the wrong impression; there was no physical relationship. She kept telling me to pretend I was meeting with a ghost. The only time we touched was that first time I saw her, when I had reached out for her cheek to make sure she wasn't just an illusion.

Although that doesn't change the fact that I was betraying your mother. Like I said, she knew I hadn't forgotten about Misako. For some reason, that much was conveyed without my ever saying a word about it. That knowledge caused her a lot of suffering, but her real pain came from something else entirely. After everything that had happened, the family decided together that they couldn't let Misako live, but your mother was convinced she'd been the first to make the suggestion. She couldn't help agonizing over whether she'd done so because she was attracted to me, because somewhere in her heart she'd considered her sister an obstacle.

Your mother was important to me, and as her husband I loved her as best I could, but it wasn't enough to release her from her anguish. I think you could understand that, Ryosuke, since you read the notebooks. I couldn't feel for anyone else the way I felt for Misako. How can I put it… Misako was more than just a woman. It didn't make a difference whether we slept or were even with each other or not.

Dad paused, having glanced several times at the clock on the cupboard, and just then we heard the sound of someone opening the front door. Yohei jolted in his seat. There was a soft glow in Dad's eyes. He continued speaking as though nothing had happened.

We last met during *Tanabata* this year, just a few months ago. I told her that your mother had died. I knew by then there wouldn't be another *Tanabata*, not with my physical condition. Misako took the news calmly.

Do you remember when we all went out to a crab dinner, back when your mother was still around? It was the first time you brought Chie to see us, Ryosuke, and you even picked up the tab. I took Misako one of the photos from that day. She stared at it in complete silence.

The entryway was still. Our visitor was waiting very patiently, not uttering a word.

My throat was totally parched. There was a glass of beer on the table before me, but I couldn't even pick it up to take a sip.

Ever since then I wondered if it might come to this. You know, Misako coming to pick me up, and the two of us taking a trip together. I've been looking forward to it, and waiting the whole time since then.

Misako's just through there, Ryosuke. If you don't want to see her, I'll take her away somewhere, and you and Yohei can leave while we're out. I said we're going on a trip but you don't need to worry about my health, she's going to take me by car. Without a license of course, since she can't officially get one. It shouldn't be a problem though, she tells me she's been doing it for years.

So, Ryosuke…what do you want to do?

I got up from my chair and tottered into the corridor.

She was standing quietly with one foot on the entryway ledge, a black silhouette set against the light streaming through the frosted glass in the door behind her. Yet I immediately realized who it was. Halfway through Dad's story, I hadn't been able to stop myself from thinking it might be her. She'd been by my side for some time, always there to lend quiet support when things had been their most difficult.

"Hello, Ryosuke. I'm here to pick up your father," Ms. Hosoya said, her voice the same as always as she bobbed her head in greeting.

I couldn't come up with a reply. I just stood there, staring at her like a fool. Yohei emerged from the kitchen and wordlessly put a hand on my shoulder. We stood facing Ms. Hosoya. I thought, stupidly, that he wouldn't know who she was. Then I remembered I'd once shown him a photo of her on my phone.

At some point, Dad had joined us. His hand was gripping my other shoulder.

"Surprised, Ryosuke?" he said.

In the next moment I remembered something that made my heart freeze solid. Mom had been there when I'd shown that photo to Yohei. She'd seen Ms. Hosoya, too.

"Dad… The photo. I-I showed it to Mom…"

"I know. From that free trial day or something at the cafe in the spring—Misako was in it. Your mother told me. I hadn't known about it so it was a surprise for me, too, although I'd told Misako you were planning to open this unusual cafe. Your mother said she recognized Misako immediately. Misako's appearance had changed a lot, and she was wearing glasses like she is right now, but your mother still knew. Probably because Misako was always in her thoughts."

Mom and Yohei were both allergic to animal hair, so neither had visited Shaggy Head. That was why I'd thought to show them the photo. Although I had taken a few casual shots, Ms. Hosoya had only ended up in one of them, and in profile at that. Maybe I should have realized that was strange. Instead, I actually pointed her out, both to Yohei and to Mom. *This is Ms. Hosoya, the one I talk about all the time.*

"So that was…that was why Mom looked so afraid…before the accident."

"Afraid? No, you're wrong about that. Emiko—your mother—told me she was relieved, from the bottom of her heart. She looked overjoyed. She told me nothing else mattered now. Her sister, who she thought she'd essentially killed, was alive. I suppose it's true she was a bit more distracted after that, as though some knot inside of her had loosened. And when she had the accident, wandering out like that before the light changed…"

For a while, Dad, Yohei, and I stood there in the narrow hallway just outside the kitchen, looking at Ms. Hosoya as she looked at us.

Finally, Dad took his hand from my shoulder and stepped forward. "Right, it's time to go. Give my love to Chie and

Miyuki. You'll find my bankbook and the deeds to the house and all that stuff inside the small bureau in the living room. I'll leave it to the two of you to work out the details."

We followed after him as though we were sleepwalking. He sat on the ledge at the entryway and tied the laces on his well-worn shoes. As he stood up Ms. Hosoya reached out to him. He paused briefly, touched her hand, then gripped it, letting her take his weight as he rose.

"How's the weather looking?"

"Spots of showers, but it's sometimes nice to drive on days like this."

"That's true. And I'm feeling pretty good today."

They exchanged smiles. They looked almost painfully innocent, like a couple getting ready for an excursion. I would recall those expressions many, many times.

Still supporting Dad, Ms. Hosoya turned to face me. "My apologies for not discussing this with you beforehand, but I'm taking the cafe's car. My resignation letter is with Chie, along with payment for the car."

"Resignation? But you can't... That's so sudden..." I couldn't shake my usual mindset of thinking like her boss.

"Everything will be just fine. Look after the place with Chie."

My mother and Ms. Hosoya: I couldn't reconcile the two as one person. I was still so stunned that I couldn't take my eyes off her familiar features. It almost felt like another face might rise to the surface if I watched for long enough. But no matter how long I stared I only saw Ms. Hosoya, her expression as placid as ever.

"Could you help us with the door, please?" she asked.

I stepped through the entranceway and rested my hand on the front door as requested. She briefly stepped away from Dad and came over to me, quickly whispering into my ear, "Don't worry about Chie's negatives. I got them all back and already disposed of them."

It came to me in a flash. In that brief moment I was back there again, the blood scattered across the window and pooled on the floor mat of Shiomi's car vivid in my mind's eye.

That had been Ms. Hosoya's doing. Was it possible? There was the sharp glare she'd given me when I'd impulsively said that I would kill him. The admonishment in her voice when she told me I couldn't think like that.

Did she, aware of my plan, kill him in order to prevent me from doing it? Or had she intended to kill him either way? Did Shiomi really ask that she bring the money? Or did she lie on the spur of the moment to stop me from getting near him?

In any case, now that she'd told me she had gotten rid of the negatives, the only conclusion I could draw was that she killed him. I suppose she lied to me about the meeting time Shiomi had given her. She must have put Chie to bed, gone to the lookout at the real hour, and arranged things so I would arrive after it was all done.

Before she took Dad's hand again, Ms. Hosoya removed her glasses and put them in her bag. She probably didn't wear them when they were together, or perhaps, at any other time except when she was working at the cafe.

Ms. Hosoya and Dad walked past me, practically brushing the tip of my nose. Yohei came up to my side, and when I looked his way I saw that he was weeping quietly. The car, parked just beyond the front gate, was wet from the drizzle.

I saw the familiar logo of Shaggy Head on the side, painted red, black, and yellow. It's impossible to rent or buy a car without owning a license. This was the only car Ms. Hosoya could use. She'd probably used it on the night of the murder, too.

I wondered what she had done with Shiomi's body. The car was usually loaded with a collapsible cart big enough to carry cages for large dogs. A woman could move something heavy around using that cart. She must have wheeled the corpse away, probably not so much to cover up the murder, but so I wouldn't have to see the body. She would have considered the blood-filled car enough to assure me he was definitely dead. Most importantly, she would have had no choice but to leave one of the cars at the scene—Shiomi's or the cafe's.

"What's this, Yohei? You're crying again?" Dad chuckled, turning back once he got to the car.

"But this…this is crazy. You don't even have any luggage." It was the first time he'd spoken in a while.

"Yohei, don't worry," Ms. Hosoya said soothingly. "The car's been properly packed with food, drinks, warm clothes, and memories of your mother."

"Ha ha, indeed, memories of our loved ones make up the lion's share of baggage. That's the one thing we can't leave behind even if we want to. No choice but to carry them wherever we go."

Did she bury the body somewhere in the mountain? Or did she take it home and deal with it in a more meticulous manner—during the three days she'd taken off to make sure no one would ever find it? It seemed as though I would never get the chance to ask.

Ms. Hosoya opened the passenger door and Dad very carefully eased himself inside. I held on to Yohei so he wouldn't run over and stop him. Could I do anything else?

"Now then, boss, Yohei, take care of yourselves."

I knew there were things I had to say to her that would be irreparable not to, but not a single word came to mind. As I gazed at her, wishing for my eyes to communicate something of my thoughts, Ms. Hosoya broke into a smile. When she smiled, standing there with her hair growing damp in the cold rain, that phantom of my youthful mother, wearing her summer dress, her arms bare, carrying a white handbag, flickered into view.

My darling Ryosuke.

The face of my mother—nothing more than an elusive apparition a day earlier—resolved for the first time into a distinct image, enveloping me with a tender smile. I stared back, unblinking, my mouth hanging open. I forgot to breathe.

Then Ms. Hosoya smoothly swept into the driver's seat and closed the door behind her.

"All right. I'm trusting you boys to look after Gran," Dad reminded, and spent a while looking at both of us in turn. Then he diverted his gaze and swung the door shut.

That was the true moment of our parting from Dad.

The car window was still rolled down, but that seemed to be the moment Dad severed all his ties. He had relinquished his final attachment to staying alive, cut off nostalgic longing for the home he had lived in for so many years, and even shed his feelings for us. In a space that contained nothing except the two of them and their memories, he was once again Ms. Hosoya's—my mother's—*you.*

"Now, then. Where to?" he said.

"Anywhere. Wherever you want."

Even as the window slid shut with a quiet noise he never turned back towards us. "Let's see. How about…"

I couldn't hear the rest of the sentence. I could see them nodding together through the closed window, enjoying themselves. When they pulled away, a stream of white exhaust fumes trailed in the rain. The car headed down the narrow residential street and disappeared around a corner. It was gone in less than ten seconds.

Yohei was crying so hard that I put an arm around his back. We stood shoulder to shoulder for a long time, just gazing at the wet, deserted asphalt.

About the Author

Mahokaru Numata was born in 1948 in Osaka, Japan, the daughter of a Buddhist priest. She married a priest, but later divorced and took holy orders herself. She went on to run her own construction consulting firm before making her literary debut in 2004 with the prize-winning novel *If September Could Last Forever*. Known for weaving strong threads of sexuality and violence into her stories, she is also recognized for her insightful explorations of such universal themes as love and hate, light and darkness, and the mysteries of human nature.